I'm too young to be this old,
My name is different, I was told,
But until I find myself, Oh God,

THIS FACE BEHIND I HIDE

A historical novel by

Arpad J. Gergely

Cover artwork by

Zsuzsanna Gergely Putnam

This Face Behind I Hide

This book is a work of fiction based of historical events. Its characters and some of its places are imaginary, others are real.

Library of Congress Cataloguing-in-Publication Data
Arpad J. Gergely
This Face Behind I Hide

ISBN – 10   1-4243-0053-3
ISBN – 13   978-1-4243-0053-2

Published and Distributed by:
Arpad J. Gergely
275 Winter Haven Lane
Brownsville, Texas 78526
956-831-4569
ajgergely@juno.com

Cover artwork by: Zsuzsanna Gergely Putnam
Manufactured by King Printing Company, Inc.
Lowell, MA 01852
www.adibooks.com

First printing 2006
10 9 8 7 6 5 4 3 2 1

**To my lifetime partner and first critique of this work,
My dear wife:**

This book was promised to You a very long time ago.
At the time when we placed our names together in
matrimony,
Kazinczy Nagy Ilona and Gergely Arpad, our initials read:
KNIGA, the Russian word for BOOK.
So, here it is. The book with a little bit of me, and a little bit
of You.
Sorry that it took me so long!

ACKNOWLEDGMENTS

A grateful appreciation is given here to all my friends who assisted in the creation of this work. To Skip Johnston, whose restless red pen, as well as to Diana and Dave Young's blue pencil that removed most of the linguistic impurities; to Bill Hudson, whose trusting interest shaped this work to fruition; and to Diane Kamperman, whose advise and encouragement helped though the long process of publishing. I am thankful to Bill Smith, who so graciously solved the mysterious process of bringing modern technology down to my desktop.

But it is also proper to give acknowledgement to you too, Dear Reader, for your indirect financial support to some causes close to our hearts. The story here had to be told to give tribute and memorial to the 200,000 Hungarian refugees who were forced to flee their country. Today, they hopefully have a better life, but they, and their descendants, are separated from our homeland, and are spread out around the globe. So, to help and support their ongoing efforts to learn or retain their mother tongue and culture, some of the income from this book goes to the many Hungarian cultural institutions that keep our language alive and well.

Finally, here is a long overdue heartfelt thanks for all that great support we refugees have received from the many Societies of the International Red Cross in general, and the American Red Cross in particular, for they are the Good Samaritans who are first at the scene of major disasters made by nature or by man. We are so glad you came to our rescue.

Arpad J. Gergely
Brownsville, Texas
March 2006

PROLOGUE

At the end of the war of all wars in 1945, the great Super Powers of the world gathered to arrange retribution by generous rewards to the winners, and severe punishments to the losers. Borders were shifted to benefit some countries and to chastise others. Many thousands of people woke up one morning suddenly in a foreign country. Military troops that survived the bloodshed were marching through foreign lands to POW camps, others stayed on conquered lands to police a peaceful recovery from the devastation of the war. American and British soldiers camped all over Western Europe while Russians occupied all the land east of the Elba River. The world of European civilization was divided into two distinct sides that eventually engaged in a seemingly bloodless Cold War. The Soviet Union embraced its satellites of small countries to build International Communism. Hungary, at the crossroads of Europe, having lost two thirds of its territory, succumbed under the control of yet another foreign power.

Throughout history Hungarians bowed to one alien repression after another. The Tartars nearly destroyed them in the fifteenth century; the Turks conquered them in the sixteenth and stayed there for 150 years. Western powers chased the Ottoman Empire back to its borders, but now they stayed on and ruled over Hungary until 1848, when destitution and courage brought on a short lived bloody revolution. The Russian Tsar helped the Austrian Kaiser to crush the uprising. Military might suppressed insurgency, and life went on without much change, even if Latin was mandated as their official language. They toiled on small farms for a meager survival; they slaved under their feudal overlords.

A hundred years later another attempt was made to plant new ideas into stubborn Hungarians. Many centuries of feudalism, the oppression of the rich over the poor, the control over the minds by religion, the millions of serfs supporting a few aristocrats' high class living had to be changed. At first, socialism gave hope for a better existence. When in 1948 the Communist Party finagled control of Hungary's government, the meek really inherited that small part of the earth. The rest of the population suffered its consequences. Private property and all commerce were nationalized until everyone served only one ruler, the Communist Party. And under the protective arms of Russian military, all rights were revoked under new laws; all human endeavors were prohibited, unless they were permitted. Socialism was enjoyed only by a few, feared by the rest. Informers entangled society at the workplace, at schools, everywhere to report on insurgency and enhance their lot. Neighbors kept their eyes and ears on neighbors, children squealed on their parents. A negative comment on the political system, a sneak visit to a church brought down the wrath of the government on the accused, and promotion for the accuser.

There were no rebels to blow up Russian soldiers with roadside bombs. The Soviet Union did not suffer any losses from insurgents. Dissidents were quickly removed from society to concentration camps, political prisons and secret death chambers by their own Hungarian KGB. The undesirables of the past regime; the intelligentsia with their educated objection to social equality; the small farmers who refused to give up their property to community agriculture were gathered up in secret, in the middle of the night, to never be heard of again. Even their families had suffered because they dared not to accept a different political system to replace their old beliefs.

By the year 1956, more and more people began to question their suppressed conditions. Ripe for a change, a small nation in Central Europe rebelled against their own government to demand human rights, to shake the yoke of foreign occupation, to gain some personal freedoms. So, for a short 12 days, the glimmer of hope for democracy bloomed in Hungary. But, as the whole world watched in disbelief, Soviet tanks crushed again those who rejected communism. By the slogan of Lenin, 'Who is not with us, is against us,' every excuse was used to justify the force-feeding of communism to the tiny country behind the Iron Curtain. Even if it would be better for them, even if half the world believed that it was the right way for them to live, they objected with sticks and Molotov cocktails and home made bombs. The death toll rose to many thousands on both sides of the conflict, still, the rebels lost.

In the aftermath, more than 200,000 Hungarians fled their country to escape retaliation. Young and old;

IV

strong and feeble; good and evil were running away to neighboring Austria, taxing another small country's ability to help so many refugees.

They were called *fluhtlings* now, refugees in German, but suddenly they were free. Free to go and choose democracy in America, or monarchy in England. Free to take a rare opportunity in their lives to change their names, ages, religions, if they had one, and even their marital status to alter their past, to suit their present, to modify their future. They could change everything but their faces. So, behind these faces we find some miserable, weary, sometimes wicked lives hidden by new official documents.

1

A burst of gunfire woke her. She heard the distinct sound of bullets ricocheting off the stucco of the outside wall behind her head. Erika Molnar had slept restlessly the past few nights while the fighting went on at the Killian Barracks only a few blocks away. The massive, old buildings in this part of Budapest soaked up most of the noise of the battle, but this last round of machinegun fire came from a very close range. She held her breath in dead silence. It was still dark outside and the phosphorous face of the ancient alarm clock showed ten past six. Then, at least for the time being, in this late October morning in 1956, eerie silence took over. The fighters of the Hungarian Revolution withdrew into the dark gloom.

Only Erika and her grandfather occupied the small, two-room apartment on the second floor not far from one of the main thoroughfares of the city. She had the so-called combination room, the all around place used for dining, studying or just listening to the radio. Every night she opened up the old sofa bed near the only window in the room, while her grandfather slept in the kitchen on a makeshift wooden cot that also served as a sitting bench during the day. Only breakfasts and lunches were eaten in the kitchen, but suppers were served in Erika's room, so that Radio Free Europe or Voice of America broadcasts would not be missed.

For many years there was always at least one member of the Molnar family who toiled in the small butcher shop downstairs from their flat. When the communists took over in 1948, the new government 'nationalized' the store, and graciously offered Geza Molnar the opportunity to stay on as manager, and the only employee.

Erika's father had broken ranks from the tradesmen in the family, she was told, and gone to military school. By the time Erika was two years old, he was fighting for the Axis on the Russian front of World War II. The last anyone heard, his regiment had retreated all the way back to Germany, and at the end of the war, he supposedly went to America. His wife and child never saw him again, nor could he learn about the loss of the family business. Erika's mother drowned in the Danube in the summer of 1946; her grandmother succumbed to pneumonia only two years ago.

Gunshots erupted again from far away. She kneeled up in her bed and peeked out the window. A pale streak of dawn illuminated the top of the buildings across the street, and just in front of her home, she noticed something very unusual. Two large artillery guns blocked most of the roadway, and she could hardly make out the armored truck behind the guns. The end of another truck, covered with dark, khaki canvas, was also visible in the shadow close to the wall. Uniformed figures took cover behind their vehicles, their submachine guns in firing position. From the opposite direction bullets began to fly, some hitting the brick frame of her window. Ducking low, Erika suddenly realized that again, the fighting had reached dangerously close.

'Ruskies' she whispered. Their long dark winter coats and black furry hats, the uniform of the Russian Tank Division, reminded her of the devil. She shivered, and imagined horns protruding from their temples. She crouched down and away from her bed and crawled to the kitchen. In the dim light of dawn, she noticed that her grandfather had made up his cot, and already gone down to the shop.

Normally, Erika would get up at seven, make a pot of poor men's coffee, a mix of dark roasted chicory and barley, and take some down to the store before she would leave for her sophomore classes at Arpad High School. The old man could not eat anything too early in the morning, but by the time Erika was ready with a breakfast of buttered rolls and coffee, he was hungry too. Every day, she would stop at the small grocery store down the street and pick up some fresh rolls, but during the fighting most of the stores were closed. Her coffee now had to be without milk and they only had leftover stale bread to go with it.

She put the coffeepot on the burner and waited for the hissing of gas from the pipes, because, for one reason or another, the supply lines sometimes were shut off. She washed and dressed quickly to start her day. Her hair did not need much attention; smartly she had it cut very short just before the revolution began. The boyish style added to her fifteen years, and she felt more mature with it.

Morning was now rolling in at full speed, and when she dared approach the window again, she could clearly see the Russian barricade. When the coffee was done, she wrapped all the leftover bread and a small piece of butter into a clean dishtowel. It was just enough for her grandfather, but she would say she already had hers; otherwise, he wouldn't touch it. She held the hot mug in another towel and slowly headed to the stairs.

The butcher shop had a back door opening from the courtyard, but the large corrugated steel shield that protected the front door and the store windows, opened only from the street side. The old man usually went around the building to raise the shield and unlock the glass entrance door. Then, he would pull the metal curtain half way down again until he was ready to open for business.

Erika turned into the narrow hallway and found the back door of the butcher shop still locked. She could not understand why her grandfather did not open it since it was fairly warm in the courtyard and would also let some fresh air into the shop. She placed the coffee mug and the food on the floor near the wall, shook the door handle again, and headed to the street entrance. The door in the main gate to the building was shut, but was unlocked. She opened it slowly and turned towards the corner of their street. The area was deserted, and from this point, she could not see the Russians, but she knew they would be on the other side of the building, only meters away from the front of the store. She crept along the sidewalk, her fingers lightly touching the wall as she made the slow journey to the corner. Her heart was pounding in her throat, the black-headed devils still dancing in front of her eyes.

Nearing the corner she could hear some voices, the murmur of soldiers still arranging their barricade. She took a deep breath. In three more steps, she would be at the front of the store and in two more, there would be protection behind the door of the butcher shop. She would be with her grandfather; she wouldn't have to cross the front of the building again as long as the Russians were out there.

She turned the corner, and took a full view of the street in front of the store. The open top transport car flanked the large military truck with a machine gun mounted on the top of the cab. She estimated at least a dozen soldiers to be there, most standing around an open campfire now in the middle of the pavement.

Her feet froze in their tracks and a long, noiseless scream filled her ears as she stared glassy eyed at the bundle at the bottom of the store door. She recognized the old winter coat and the worn gray hat that rolled away only a few meters from where she stood. The old man was lying on his back, his arms spread out, his fist still clenching a bundle of keys. His white working coat glared exposed in the morning light. A few streaks of gray hair on his balding head were messed up and moved slightly in the breeze. His open mouth was twisted from horror, his yellow face resting in a puddle of blood.

Within seconds she heard the disturbance she had caused. She looked up to see the machinegun spinning around on the top of the car, and she felt the mortar peeling off the brick wall and splashing against her face. The noise of the gun was still ringing in her ears as she was now running full speed down the sidewalk. Her heart pounding, she heard the loud laughter of her attackers echoing through the empty street behind her. Once in the protection of the solid doors of her building, she pressed against it with her full weight, then slowly collapsed from exhaustion.

Erika was alone in the dark entrance hall. The street behind the oak gate was quiet. She did not know how much time had elapsed since she found her grandfather's body; for she knew that he was gone, even if she had never seen anyone dead before.

She did not dare make a sound. Her tears were flowing freely down her pale cheeks, but she did not care to wipe them. She rested against the door, sitting on the cold concrete, trying not to think. But the horrible scene was hounding her, the dark fact that now she was all alone in the world could not find room in her mind. She often thought of her father in America, but even if he was alive, he was just as dead to her now, for she knew she would never see him.

Finally she got up and slowly wandered back to the apartment. She let the mug of coffee and the bread stay where she had left them, and sat on the kitchen cot in a daze. It must have been hours before she began to think again. She thought of the hundreds of freedom fighters who were dying on the streets, not here, but somewhere in a remote world, from where only the sounds of gunfire reached her. She tried to calm herself by thinking that all this fighting was only a nuisance in her life, something that made her miss school, that's all.

*   *   *

This strange but destructive war on the streets of Budapest began with a peaceful march in the afternoon of October 23, 1956. At first, a few dozen college students gathered at Petofi Square showing solidarity with the recently crushed revolt in Poland. They sang the Hungarian national anthem; listened to the recital of patriotic poems by Imre Sinkovics, the well-known actor, culminating in the decision to take their symbolic message to the statue of General Joseph Bem on the other side of the city. The renowned Polish soldier's helping Hungary's first fight for freedom over a hundred years ago deserved their tribute.

As the crowd began to move, common folks, curious shoppers, workers finishing their shifts, and schoolchildren joined the first unauthorized gathering the city had seen since communist control. More and more people crammed into the street, moving slowly towards the Danube, blocking all motorized traffic on the avenue. They started to openly question the Russian occupation of their homeland, and soon, shouts of *"Ruskies Go Home!"* grew into a loud chorus of demand. Their list also included other claims that asked for an independent Hungary, basic individual rights for free speech and gathering, unfiltered information about the western side of the world, and a multi-party political system.

For hours the multitude grew to many thousands, got louder and more assertive with every step. Word of the unusual event spread quickly throughout the city. Other groups approached the capital building, some went after media centers. A small group of excited citizens stormed the main radio station to broadcast their demands to the rest of the nation. A single shot came from the armed guards of the station, killing a fourteen year old boy. Aggression escalated on both sides. Some Hungarian soldiers on furlough ran back to their posts and returned with weapons, more than they needed. An armed, bloody revolt spread like wildfire through the streets of Budapest. Thus, by that night, the first salvo had torn a gap in the once indestructible Iron Curtain of International Socialism.

In the ensuing days Hungary's communist government and its armed Government Defense Units (AVO) used all their might to crush the growing number of insurgents. Sudden attacks came from rooftops and narrow alleys by both sides of the conflict, mostly during the dark of night. The Russian military, occupying the country since the end of World War II, hopelessly tried to bring back law and order. During the daylight hours, the warriors hid, and almost normal life emerged on the streets. A general strike called by the revolutionaries stalled most work and traffic in the surprised city. Periodically, Russian tanks and armored cars sped through the avenues, their tracks rattling with ominous noise, scaring away most uprising activities in their paths.

It wasn't really Erika's war, for she always had everything she needed. She was a good student, and learning about communism was just part of a student's life, something you had to do to become a better Hungarian. She thought of herself as being part of the working class, and she was happy that whatever life had been before she was born, had happened so long ago. She was taught in school not to want "that type" of life, and she could not understand how some people would want it so badly that they would even die for it.

Her grandfather had been ready to join the fight, if she had let him. Only her long talk about how much she needed him kept him home. She had heard his story about the family's past, but even if she could fully comprehend it, she could never feel the importance of owning property, owning one's business.

Suddenly it all came to her. She too was on the loser's side now; she too had something to fight back for. She still did not know why her grandfather had to die; only the image of his pale face on the bloody sidewalk remained. Then, she knew, she must do something about it.

She did not dare remove the body since the Russians had already shot at her before. But even if she could drag him back into the house, she could hardly bury him anywhere. Then, a strange, but natural thought occurred to her. She would cremate him! Burn him right on the spot where he had died and save his ashes. She knew of a large container of kerosene in the basement. She could sneak out at night, under the cover of darkness, and could soak the body with enough fluid to do the job. She did not think the Russians would put out the fire. All she had to do now was to wait for darkness.

It must have been way after lunchtime when she felt the first pang of hunger. Now that she had at least one important purpose in life, she knew she must nourish herself to keep up her strength. She found her grandfather's last breakfast and brought it back with the cold coffee from the hallway.

During the fighting she ventured out of the house only once, and only a block away from her home. She found that on Joseph Boulevard, where normally hundreds of pedestrians would crowd the sidewalks, there were only a few people now. Everyone was moving fast, with the fear of knowing that they could be shot at from any window or rooftop. While they were not seen, the enemy was everywhere. Some abandoned streetcars were standing on their tracks in the middle of the road; the war torn city seemed too calm in the damp and unseasonably warm late October air. Then, she heard a tank approaching. It came down on the right side of the avenue from the direction of the Danube River, its tracks clattering sparks on the worn cobblestones. Its turret closed, the thundering contraption was blindly making its way on the wide road. She retreated into a doorway.

She noticed two young boys, about her age or younger, appearing from a nearby building. As the tank passed by, suddenly the boys took after it. One quickly jumped up on the rear end and climbed up to the turret. He leaned his back against it for support, while the other boy, still running alongside, produced a green wine bottle from under his coat and carefully tossed it to his partner on the tank. In a matter of seconds, he clicked a cigarette lighter and lit the white rag that corked the bottle. He smashed the Molotov cocktail over the grill of the engine, and jumped off to the side. The gasoline went up in a roar. Flames engulfed the tank as it sped away. As the road bent in the distance,

Erika could hear the machine crashing into the side of a building. By the time of the next explosion, the young freedom fighters had disappeared into a side street.

The event had taken place only a few days ago, but it lingered sharply in her memory. She thought of her grandfather again, and the Russians at the corner of her street who took his life. Revenge fueled her otherwise numb determination to do something. A gruesome plan slowly developed in her mind. In a daze, she found a bottle of vinegar on the kitchen shelf and she slowly poured its contents down the drain. She knew of a motorcycle parked under the back stairs in their courtyard. She did not know to whom it belonged, and she did not care. She had abandoned her plans for the cremation, she wanted more than one man's funeral.

Somehow, she found the motorcycle in the darkness. She grabbed the handlebars and gently shook the machine. The precious liquid she was after sloshed around in the fuel tank. All she needed now was a way to get it out. She had never paid attention to motorcycles before, but she knew that the gasoline from the tank must flow somehow to the engine below. She found the valve and turned it. Nothing! A thin plastic tube connected the tank to the engine. She yanked out the lower end of the tube and turned the valve again. The clear liquid splashed all over the concrete floor. She quickly lifted up the vinegar bottle.

Erika waited in the dark until about nine. She did not think of anything else. She was left-handed, and she practiced in her mind how she must throw the flaming bottle, and clear at least ten meters in order to reach the Russian guns. A shiver ran down her back as she realized that she couldn't light a match in the dark without being seen by the soldiers.

She needed the quicker strike of a cigarette lighter, and her grandfather had been a smoker.

The main gate of her building squeaked no matter how slowly she tried to open it. But outside, there was not a soul in sight, only the precious darkness. She took her shoes off and put them in her coat pockets. The thin socks she was wearing quickly transferred the wet coolness of the sidewalk to her feet, but she did not feel it. Perspiration shone on her forehead as she clutched the bottle in her bent arm. The few meters seemed to take forever to cover, but she finally reached the corner. She could hear the Russians talking; the campfire threw their shadows across the pavement. She knew that at least some of them had their backs to her.

She crept down on the sidewalk, as close as possible to the wall, and began to crawl. Her enemy was busy eating late supper, and if there was a sentry there, she did not see him. She lifted the bottle in front of her, moving it a few centimeters at a time. Little by little, she had reached her grandfather's body. She held her tears back as she searched his pockets. She had no idea where she would find his cigarette lighter, if he had it on him at all. She held her breath and nearly forgot to take another, for the first pocket was empty. She pulled hard on the cold, stiff mass that once was the only living family in her life. She twisted his body to its side and finally retrieved the lighter. Geza Molnar painlessly slumped back to the ground.

She slowly pulled her hand free and came up to her knees. Her bottle of destruction rested on the ground between her legs. She changed to a crouching position to be able to stand up quicker. She took a final glance at the distance behind her to judge escape time, then forward to look for a target. The gaping shadow of the open rear end of the truck appeared to be the closest.

There were no practice throws or even a second chance to light the bomb. The lighter must work on the first try, or she was doomed. Her hands shook as she rearranged the rag corking the bottle. It was bone dry. Her careful handling of the bomb did not make enough movement for the gasoline to reach the top. She tilted the bottle and waited impatiently. She felt the cold wetness in her palm; she knew she was ready. She clutched the lighter between her fingers and struck the gear. A small flicker came to life, and then a bigger one as the rag caught on fire. She dropped the lighter and rising tall, grabbed the bottle with both hands. She swung back, then forward with all her might.

She did not wait for the flames to engulf the back of the truck. She knew from the commotion that the solders had discovered her, but by then, she was safely behind the corner of the building. The balls of her feet struck hard on the concrete, sending painful shocks to her brain with every step. She had reached the gate to her building when she heard the first explosion. Then another, and another. The sky was bright behind her and the tremor of a collapsing building shook the ground. She must have hit an ammunition truck.

She slammed the heavy door shut with all her weight. Her back pressed hard against it as she slowly began to catch her breath. Then, from the other end of the dark entry hall, she saw the figure of a large man approaching.

"What's happening out there?" the voice trembled.

She recognized the face. The Superintendent was visibly shaken. He took the responsibility of keeping the revolution out of his building very seriously. Looking at Erika, he felt the fighting coming right through the door.

"What are you doing out there in curfew time?" he demanded to know. There were no more explosions outside; only the crackling of fire could be heard over the screams of some of the soldiers. It seemed there were survivors of the attack, and if there were, there were also witnesses.

The man leaned over her now. "You reek of gasoline," he shouted, "you are one of them! What did you do out there?"

She could not say a word. Slowly she passed around the man and began to walk to the stairs. "They will get you for this Erika Molnar!" she heard his voice echoing in the corridor, "I'll make sure they do!" She did know even before she left her building that night that he was right. Now she was one of them, whoever they were. She also felt relieved; she did her part as expertly as she could. What started out as a nomadic, tribal funeral for her grandfather, turned out to be a revolutionary attack on the enemy. What would happen with the bodies, the body of her grandfather, was now beyond her capabilities. Her job was done now, and with that, for Erika Molnar, the Hungarian Revolution of 1956 ended. She sat against the wall on the old cot in her kitchen waiting for the consequences of her deed. That's where Frank found her.

2

When Frank Bartha arrived, he found the apartment door to Erika's place wide open. She was sitting on the kitchen cot, propped up against the wall, staring into the air. He closed the door and lightly kissed her forehead.

"What's with you?"

"He's gone," she said quietly, "Grandpa is gone."

"What?"

"He is dead! They shot him."

Before she could say anything more, the kitchen door burst open and two Russian soldiers jumped in, ready to fire.

"Pashly, pashly!" one motioned with his weapon to move on. They silently walked down the stairs and out to the sidewalk. About a dozen people in the building were rounded up and lined against the wall.

"I don't want to die," Erika whispered, "I don't want to die." There were no tears, just jerky sobs of fear, as the frightened soul was trying to shake loose from the petrified body. She stood behind Frank and wrapped her arms around him, her fingers dug into his chest, her face buried deep into the back of his winter coat. Her frail body pressed against the crude stone wall behind her as she tried pulling him ever closer.

"One of you is a mass murderer," the man in the leather coat screamed, nervously pacing the sidewalk in front of the frightened lineup. "And in five minutes, you will tell me who! Because in five minutes, we will shoot one of you, and will keep shooting again and again, until I find out!"

Frank's eyes followed every move the lieutenant made. He could not remember the man's name, but he had seen his face in his father's office enough times to recognize him even in the dark. Frank's father was the District Political Officer of the AVO. While the uniformed men were responsible to protect the communist government from its enemies within its borders, Captain Bela Bartha kept the spirit of communism alive and well in the hearts and minds of the enlisted protectors. It was a crucial responsibility and he did his job as a matter of gratitude for the good life his position ensured for him and his family. At this minute, his only son was facing death from the very same forces he had supported for all these years.

Frank knew that at any minute he would be recognized. While he could not move, his broad shoulders were desperately trying to hide his girlfriend in the blind hope that he could stop the bullets before they reached her, or just cushion the impact to make death soft, less painful.

He counted five Russians standing coldly in the middle of the street, their sub-machineguns protruding darkly in front of their winter uniforms. To his right the wall ended about ten meters away. Behind it, he saw the dark opening of a side street. 'Ten meters between life and death,' he thought, 'ten physically impossible meters.' No way could he sprint out and leap the distance to the protective shadows behind the building before the Russian bullets would cut him down. No way could he do it, let alone drag Erika along. It would be a foolish suicidal move.

The lieutenant stopped suddenly and shined a flashlight in Frank's face. "Whom are you hiding behind you, young man," he said stepping closer. "Oh, Comrade Bartha?" he shouted in surprise, "What are you doing here? Are you here to crush this counter-revolution, or was I right to suspect all along you being a traitor?" He lowered the light and stepped aside. His soldiers took the signal and suddenly, a sub-machinegun burst up. The deafening rattle echoed through the empty street. Frank saw the lieutenant's arm go up in the air, a signal to stop the firing. In the silence that followed, Frank could hear the thump as the old, fat woman next to him collapsed to the ground. The sharp powder of dry mortar showered his side and his face; his ears ringing, he felt warmth and he didn't know if the blood was his or hers. He did not dare loosen his hold on Erika, or reach up to feel his aching face. The confused soldier let his weapon drop to his side. The dead body appeared only as a dark spot at the bottom of the wall. The streetlight above threw a pale yellow glow on the group; the rest of the street was deserted.

A sudden blink of the lights was followed by shattered glass clinking on the pavement. A short distance away the street fell into darkness. All the Russians hit the ground almost at the same time. They rolled in unison towards the edge of the roadbed, moving into firing position, their weapons aimed at the darkness.

The AVO lieutenant jumped into the shadows of the gate as the first Russian was hit only seconds later. An ambush of gunfire followed. The scared group of soldiers fired aimlessly into the street, toward the empty darkness from where death came in accurate simplicity.

Frank knew the time was now! The attack on the soldiers was not aimed on the civilian lineup and only stray bullets could endanger their escape. He felt the soft body of the old woman move under his rushing feet. Then came the street corner and the dive. He fell carefully so Erika would land on him. He felt no pain.

Bursts of gunfire echoed through the dark street behind them. The small side street between the tall gray buildings was also unlit. Breathlessly, they made their way along the worn sidewalks, dodging low windowsills, keeping close to the walls. At the next intersection Frank glanced back. He heard the noise of engines roaring on the main road they had just left. Then, the gunfire subsided; only shouts and the drum of heavy footsteps filled the air. He tried the first gate they reached but it was locked. There was no sense knocking; no one would open at this time of the night.

They ran aimlessly door-to-door, block after block, but not one of the buildings was open. Budapest, torn apart by the revolution, was closed up for the night. The ancient, massive apartment buildings had only one opening to the streets, protected by a heavy main gate that had a small service door for pedestrians. A long, large corridor usually entered into a center court of concrete or cobblestone, into which opened all the living quarters on four sides and all of the five or six stories. Above the ground level a narrow walkway surrounded the court on all floors with stairwells in the corners. Usually, an open shaft elevator filled one of the stairwells near the entrance of the building.

The buildings were under the care of a Superintendent. In peacetime, he would lock the front gate for the night at eleven sharp and that door would remain closed until five in the morning. During this period, it was customary for tenants, who had to stay out after closing time, to wake up the caretaker who let them enter for a nominal fee, or 'gate money.' By the fourth night of the revolution in 1956, the gates to all the apartments in the capital were closed at night, and the Superintendents could not be awakened.

The sounds of war were getting further away now. Frank realized with relief, that at least for the time being, they were not being followed. Erika stopped and leaned against the wall.

"I can't go any further," she gasped, and let herself slide to the ground. Frank bent over her, also panting.

"We must," he whispered. "We can't stay here. You know they will kill us on sight if they catch up with us." She bowed her head in agreement, but didn't move. Her strength gave out, and she knew she wouldn't be able to continue their flight without at least a few minutes of rest.

Frank nervously scanned the area. Not far away, he spotted a cellar window. The iron cage held on to the concrete under his vigorous shakes. There was no way to enter through there. He ran to the end of the building and carefully peered into the next street. It was a larger avenue, one he was not familiar with. A short distance away he noticed an entrance to an underground restroom. He ran back to his girl.

"Come, come," he muttered in a soft voice, "there is a way to keep out of sight."

The public toilets in the city always had two entrances, one end for males and the other for females, with a small utility room between the sections for the attendant and her supplies. The attendants, usually older women, would clean the toilets from time to time, but normally, they would spend their day in this tiny room, their doors open to both sides, and collect a small fee that was subscribed by city authorities for the use of the facilities.

The place was deserted now. A strong stench of ammonia filled the damp air; filth and debris covered the stone floors. At first, he neither knew, nor cared, on which side of the restroom they entered.

Erika gagged from the odor. "We'll get used to it," he reassured her. "We must spend the rest of the night here," He glanced at his wristwatch. It was near midnight, and in a few minutes, it would be the last day of October in 1956.

He let the girl rest against the wall, and went over to the other end of the room. The attendant's cubicle was locked. He leaned against it and rattled the door handle. It was weak, but it held. He leaned back, and kicked it with the bottom of his shoe. The door smashed open. He turned on the light switch and looked around. The place was not much bigger than a broom closet. Several dirty pails were lined up under a half round wall sink. A few mops leaned against the wall. The other half of the room was filled with a makeshift cot. The bedding consisted of an old army blanket that covered an ancient straw mattress. Under the wooden contraption he found small paper boxes filled with torn up old bed sheets, the attendant's cleaning implements.

Erika collapsed on the cot. She leaned against the stone wall and pulled up her shaky legs, almost sitting on them. Frank tried to close the broken door in vain. He finally placed a garbage can against it to hold it closed and also dropped on the cot.

They sat there quietly for a few minutes, listening in the still night. The noises of the world above were shut out. The dirty bulb dangling from the ceiling gave a dim light, and he could hardly see her face. It was red from the running and

the excitement, a color that slowly faded away as she began to relax.

'What now?' he thought. The place was deserted and safe for the time being, but as the day breaks, they must move on. He knew he couldn't go back to his college dormitory. He entered his junior year at the prestigious Karl Marx University just weeks before all this turmoil started. The school specialized in political science, communist political science for sure, and groomed not only the future leaders of Hungary, but accepted students from all the other satellite countries of the Soviet Union as far away as North Korea.

Captain Bartha was one of the charter students of the university; it was just logical that his only son should follow his steps.

The whole ancestry of the Bartha family came from peasant stock small farmers. Tiny properties on the Great Plains region of Hungry supported their meager lives for generations. To join the Communist Party was Frank's father's way out of hard work that could not ease their poverty. He was a likely candidate to enter the political arena and he was anxious to serve and please the working class movement. He saw salvation and a great future. Unfortunately, the vigorous climbing of the ladder to the top of this new social order came with unavoidable side effects. He lost his wife in a divorce. She could not endure the rigors and strain of her husband's hierarchy, so she left the government owned big house on Rozsadomb where most of the new elite lived, and went back to the Great Plains.

Frank also left the spacious home in his first year of college. Not that he wasn't comfortable or happy, but the Party dictated training in self-preservation that forced him to stand on his own feet. Thus, dormitory living was the only choice. In a small room with three roommates, he struggled with the long-winded dissertations of Marx and Lenin on the great future of the proletariat, and Stalin's instructions on the proper steps to take to assure that future. When he left his room two days ago, the building was engulfed in flames, and he knew there was no attempt made to put the fire out. Going home to his father was also out of the question. The lieutenant, if he was still alive, probably reported him by now. He knew, if not in his heart, that he was involved in this revolution, at least deep enough not to accept, not without questions anyway, the side his father supported. All he knew was that in the next few hours he must make a decision that would change his life. He already felt, that the girl he had just rescued would take a major part in it.

The small bulb in the restroom flickered from power surges. Frank slowly reached out and his hand gently covered Erika's face. With his other hand he motioned towards the ceiling of their small hiding place from where muffled voices and echoes of heavy footsteps could be heard. He jumped up and turned off their light. They sat motionless in the dark, holding their breath.

Two men entered the underground public toilet. Frank quietly rose up and peered through the crack of the door he had broken earlier. He saw civilians in heavy winter jackets, appearing to be factory workers, and not soldiers. Their backs were towards him as they were urinating, engaged in casual conversation, talking about an old gas stove one was rigging up in a garage. Peacetime conversation, although both were carrying Russian made submachine guns, loosely dangling off their shoulders behind their backs. As one of them turned, taking a cigarette out of the corner of his mouth, Frank noticed he was wearing the red-white-green armband of the Revolution.

Erika came up behind him, but he gently pushed her back. He did not want her to spy on men in a toilet. Not that she wanted to; simple curiosity got her off the cot.

"Now look at that," one of the men exclaimed, "some jerk broke into the shithouse." He pointed to the smashed service door. "For God sake, what can they find down here?"

"Let's see," the other stepped closer, buttoning up his pants.

"Hell, no," said the first one, "if there was anything to take, it's already gone. Besides, let's go, it stinks in here."

"This is a trap," Frank said turning the light back on when the men left. "We must get out of here."

"What about the other door," Erika commented, "the women's side."

"I don't want to break any more doors down," he said. "I must find a better place for us to hide. Will you be all right for a few minutes?" He left without her answer.

A few blocks away he found a closed up newsstand booth at the edge of the sidewalk. The small wooden structure had windows only on the side towards the buildings, protected by heavy wire mash and a padlock. Its door at the end was unlocked. Cheap paperback books were displayed on narrow shelves around the small cubicle, and a chair was its only furnishing. Through the long days of the revolution no news service was in operation, nor were there any customers to buy their products. Under the service counter, Frank thought, seemed to be enough space for them to hide until daybreak.

When he got back to the restrooms a stooped figure of a soldier stood in the small service room. His left shoulder and half of his back was covered with blood. In his right hand, Frank could see the official AVO handgun aimed at Erika.

"No!" he screamed as he dove onto the man's back. The soldier collapsed under Frank's weight, and fell head first towards the cot, stretching his uninjured arm out for protection on his landing. As Frank rolled over the man's head, the gun spun out of the weak hold and landed near the cot.

"Grab the gun!" Frank shouted as he jumped up. Within a second he was there too, taking hold of the weapon, his back securely against the wall. He trained the muzzle on the soldier on the floor, but the man was motionless, his face slightly turned on the dirty concrete, his eyes closed.

"Did you kill him?" Erika gasped standing on the cot now, unable to move.

"I don't think so," he said, waiting for the soldier to jump up. When nothing happened, he began to move closer, straining his eyes in the semi-darkness, ready like a cat, to react to the slightest provocation.

"You check if he's alive," he said to Erika, "while I hold the gun on him."

"I can't tell if he is dead," she whispered, "I'm afraid to touch him."

"Then you hold the gun, and I'll check."

She was ready to cry, in part from the scare she had just gone through, and from being tired and cold, and now this. Shaking in her whole body, she held on to the gun with both hands, holding on tight, her palm covering the trigger. She knew she would not fire that weapon, even if her life depended on it. She had done enough killing for a lifetime.

Frank placed one hand on the side of the soldier's neck, with his other one tightened in a fist, a ready weapon in case he needed it. Finding a weak pulse on the motionless body he concluded instinctively, that the man had passed out from the sudden pain of his injuries. Frank held on and turned him on his back. He was young, about his age; his AVO uniform shabby on his thin body, and the light blue insignia on the shoulders of his uniform seemed to be bright from newness.

"This man needs help," he said quietly.

"We should not help the AVO."

"He's a rookie. Look, this is a brand new uniform. I bet he is still in boot camp."

"He is still an AVO."

"He is an injured man, and he is a comrade."

"Are you a comrade, Frank?"

"My father is a Party leader," he said, avoiding the question.

"Oh, my God," she exclaimed, "you are going to turn me in."

"It is too late for you to think that," he snapped back bitterly. "I think I have proved myself to you during the past few hours. I could have turned you in when we were in front of the firing squad."

"How could you, you did not know what I did."

"I was there when you ran from the explosion."

"And you went to report me. Is that it?"

"No, I went to take a long walk, to collect my thoughts, to figure out where I am or where I belong. I knew who you were, and whose side you were on, but I was not sure of myself."

"Are you now?"

"Yes, we are on the same side, you must believe me. But we cannot leave a defenseless man here dying, can we?"

"We are not out of danger ourselves either," she reminded him, "what can we do?"

Now that they understood each other, he was ready with a solution. Out of his pocket, he pulled out a small knife, and cut off the soldier's AVO insignias. "It will tell whoever finds him, at least where he does not belong anymore," he said as he flushed the material down a toilet. "This is all we can do now." They left on the light in the cubicle.

He held her hand as they made a few careful steps up the stairs. It was quiet on the streets as if the fighters had all gone to sleep or run out of ammunition. But Budapest did not sleep on that late October dawn. Those who had weapons nervously scanned the rooftops, dark gateways, and small alley openings for their prospective enemies. Those behind safe windows of their homes just watched nervously for the outcome of the fight.

By this time the battle at the radio station was over and its building was taken over by the freedom fighters. So was the Szikra Nyomda, where most of Hungary's newspapers were published. The Revolution was still being fought at certain parts of the capital where the government's forces, mainly members of the AVO, put up opposition to the small groups of freedom fighters. Russian tanks were making patrolling runs through the main avenues of the city, rushing at full throttle to avoid Molotov cocktail ambushes. At times, when these tanks appeared on the streets, people quietly moved to the side, or stepped into any open doorway until the Russians had passed.

Erika and Frank never made it to the newsstand hideout. By the time they got to Lenin Boulevard it was six in the morning. The official curfew had just ended, and as if on cue, the wide sidewalks of the avenue quickly filled with people.

"Where to now?" Frank asked almost to himself.

"I know someone in Aprofalu," she said, "we may be able to stay in that village until this is over."

"Never heard of it. Where is it?"

"Just outside the city limits, to the north of us."

"I don't have much money left," he said checking his pocket, counting the small change, hardly enough for two coffees.

"Grandpa must had have some money in the store," she said, "and I need some extra clothing too."

"You can't go back there, you would be recognized," he said.

"But you can. I'll tell you where everything is."

They made their way back to the store. Erika stayed across the street, far enough not to be seen, but still able to keep an eye on him. As if watching would keep Frank Bartha out of harm's way, holding that strange warm feeling in her heart would bring him back safely. But why wouldn't it?

3

The little butcher shop was conveniently located in the residential section of the Ninth District of Budapest. It served the immediate neighborhood with fresh cut meat and meat products coming in from distant collective farms. Of course, by the fourth day of the Revolution, only some smoked bacon and a few slabs of salt pork were available. A conscientious worker, Geza Molnar kept the shop open to provide his customers at least some meager foodstuffs while they lasted. Today was like any other day. He quietly made up his cot, so as not to disturb his granddaughter, and made his way to the bathroom. With his shaving implements, the soap brush and straight razor, he began his early morning ritual. Graying whiskers shadowed his pale face in the mirror. He had shaved off his narrow mustache after the funeral of his beloved Maria. She had died two winters ago, a lifetime ago that seemed like only yesterday. Erika had just turned into a teenager then but had come home as a middle aged woman after the ordeal of the funeral. She had been very close to Geza's wife of 34 years, perhaps too close, and took her passing very hard.

'She wasn't even her grandchild,' Geza thought, 'she wasn't!' He put down the razor, his hands shaking, his teary remembrance fogging his vision. He grabbed on to the edge of the sink with both hands, trying not to disappear in the darkness in his life that fate had so unfairly thrown at him. He was too good of a man to deserve all this. At least he thought he was. He had fought in the First World War, and worked as a butcher to feed the soldiers in the second. He could not do anything in this third conflict; he could not leave his adopted granddaughter behind.

'What adoption?' he recalled shivering. He remembered that late afternoon in May of 1944. An urgent call to go to the Klein residence forced Geza Molnar to close up the store early. He asked his wife to join him on the trip to the ritzy section of the city. Rozsadomb in the hills of Buda was on the other side of Margit Bridge, one of the few still standing in the war torn capital. The villa, fancy and elegant, was quiet when the Molnars arrived. Ringing the doorbell summoned the only servant left in the home. She opened the door and led them into the spacious living room. Erika Klein, just turned two, played nonchalantly with her porcelain doll. The Persian carpet looked like a decoration under her frail body.

"They took them! Took them both!" The young maid sobbed. "The Gestapo rounded up all the Jews in our street this morning. They said they needed Mr. Klein to dig trenches at the Russian front. They said Mrs. Klein is too good looking to wilt away in his absence. I don't know where they took her." She was mostly mumbling her report. By the end, she was sitting on the sofa stroking the hair of the toddler on the floor.

The Molnars were stunned, even if they secretly knew that the owners of their little shop could not avoid the inevitable. Genocide raised its ugly head throughout the war years. One by one, small sections of the population were screened, culled into ghettoes, tagged with bright yellow Star of David for obvious identification, then transported to unknown destinations, often under the cover of night. That it happened to the Kleins was not a matter of if, but when.

"How did they miss the baby?" Maria Molnar wanted to know.

"I guess they didn't know about her, or just wanted adults. I was playing with her in my room when it happened. I always let her parents eat breakfast by themselves. When those people came Mr. Klein made such a noisy resistance, it must have confused them." She picked up the little girl and tickled her under the chin. Erika giggled happily as all the adults cried.

"What can we do with the baby now?" Geza asked almost to himself.

"I can't take her back to my village," the maid said. "What would people say?"

"I guess we have a new child in our home," Maria Molnar stated plainly. "Please pack some of her things."

As the war rumbled through Hungary, the Molnars began to explain how their granddaughter had been orphaned in her parent's distant city. The story evolved through the years to the fine details of a soldier on the Russian front and the mother drowning in the Danube. Neighbors and customers accepted the stories, and felt sorry for the child for her tragic circumstances. Erika learned it also as she grew, and was always eager to repay the kindness and love of her grandparents. Guarded from the sad truth, she would never learn what really happened. Geza Molnar made sure of that. Washing off the shaving soap from his face he reassured it to the mirror. "She's a Molnar!"

His own tragic fate might have been spared today if he had only known that in the early morning darkness, his long stick that he used to manipulate the corrugated steel cover of the storefront, from the distance, to the nervous soldiers would look like a weapon.

*   *   *

When Frank walked the short route back to the apartment, it seemed the fight was over. At least for the moment. He found Erika's grandfather at the front of the shop, just as she had described it. He picked up his hat and covered the old man's gaping face. It hurt that he had to meet him for the first time this way.

He glanced around at the enormous devastation. The street was covered with debris, burned out military vehicles, loose brick, and mortar everywhere. Twisted metal beams dangled from the mere remnants of once stylish turn of the century structures. The stench of decaying human flesh mixed with burnt rubber and spent gunpowder invoked nausea. Big gaps in the pavement, scattered bodies of Russian solders, grown men's full figures shrunk to the size of small children from the intense heat of the explosions everywhere. A heavy dust of lime had been spread on the bodies, the first move by the Red Cross to avert disease. The white powder shone in the early morning light.

The corrugated shield of the entrance door had been torn by the blasts. What was once a large picture window was now in tiny shards strewn all over the floor inside. White ceramic tile walls were smashed in many places, smeared with blood where slabs of meat used to hang. Frank realized that anything edible had been ransacked from the store, but he found the old cash register in the corner intact. With the help of a cleaver he pried it open. The drawer exposed only a handful of coins.

As he turned to leave, he noticed a small open box under the counter. Some rumpled paper currency lay in the makeshift container. A piece of wax paper with barely readable scribbling lay next to the box. "We are hungry but we don't steal! This is all the money we have! God save our country!" Slowly, Frank began to put the money in his pocket. He opened the back door and entered the dark corridor. He did not bother to close the shop door behind him.

The apartment was still wide open. As the AVO rounded up the residents of the small court the previous night, closing up homes was not a priority. By now electricity was turned off in the entire city, and Frank made his way slowly through the dim kitchen. Searching for food was the first step of his mission. He found only a small jar of marmalade and two cans of factory-made goulash that could be eaten without cooking. A canvas shopping bag held his find nicely.

The combination room felt like a sanctuary, a hallowed place of a girl he loved who now needed his protection. A gentle feminine scent made him blush. In his nineteen years he never had been in a room like this. And now he must look for things that normally cover girl's figures. Blouses and underwear, stockings and skirts, only two of each, he was told to get, but now they were important for a possible long journey.

A journey to where? He didn't have to go anywhere. He had not done anything to feel guilty for or worry about punishment. He had just come to Erika's place to pick her up and take her to the movies once or twice. In the turmoil of this 'counter-revolution,' he came to make sure that she was all right. Maybe there was more to that too. At least now it was his obligation, his chevalier duty to make sure that she wouldn't be harmed. At least until this whole miserable confusion was over.

In the mean time, he must gather things he could find for the trip, even if it was only to Aprofalu, wherever that place was. A short trip until things quieted down. He knew he must go there with her; he also knew that he could not go home to his father, not after his association with the *Enemies of the State*, not with a naïve teenager who acted out of a terrible impulse, a misguided move in the wrong direction. Regardless, here they were, Erika and Frank, off the path of righteousness, the course they were taught, trained and pressured to follow. For the moment, all they needed was to find a place to hide.

Frank was getting too involved with his thoughts and worries of their future to pay any more attention to his shyness. He packed her things into the shopping bag as he found them, glancing briefly at the small-framed picture on the top of the bureau, the picture of a young skinny girl in an all white dress, a cross in her clasped hands, wrapped gently with the beads of a rosary. It was a visible record of Erika's confirmation, not a beloved sight for someone coming from a confirmed communist family. 'We are confirmed too,' Frank thought, 'only to Karl Marx and Joseph Stalin. We had a celebration too, when the government placed a red scarf to decorate our necks.' He was indoctrinated also. To follow the teachings of these men, to believe in the power of the proletariat, a peasant like him with the coalition of the workers of the world would make his life exceptionally good. He turned the photograph face down so as not to embarrass anyone further.

It seemed that his mission was accomplished when Mother Nature called. He found the small toilet closet and relieved himself. A hardwood, polished box covered the otherwise unattractive water tank hanging high up on the wall. As he reached out to activate the flushing mechanism, its chain broke and dropped on his clenched fist. Embarrassed, he quickly tried to reconnect it with its lever. For a more comfortable position, Frank stepped on the toilet cover.

At first, it seemed he damaged the whole tank. The cover shifted to the side and he wasn't able to move it back. A small plastic bag was in the way. Inside the bag, he could make out a packet of folded paper held together by a rubber band. Totally neglecting his original purpose now, Frank sat on the toilet, nervously opening the package. 'I am intruding into other peoples lives," he thought, but what if his discovery held the now much needed money for their traveling expense.

There was no money in the packet. Instead, it held wrinkled and yellowed sheets of paper, some form of documents that he spread out on his lap; a 1918 discharge paper from the Austrian-Hungarian Army of one Sergeant Geza Molnar; right below it, bordered with wide black margins, the notification of Maria Molnar's burial date and place; a marriage certificate of the Molnar's also in 1918; and another marriage license of Sarah and Emanuel Klein, marked as a merchant, dated 1939. The last document in the package was a birth certificate of one Erika Klein, on May 5, 1941, a daughter of Sarah and Emanuel Klein, all Israelites.

Frank jumped up and ran to the front room. The confirmation photograph in his hands, he tried to make sure he was looking at the same girl. In disbelief he made his way back to the toilet, repacked the documents and secured the tank cover. A voice from behind startled him, but could not overwhelm his mental confusion.

"Well, well, Comrade Bartha! We meet again. I was hoping I'd find you here." The AVO lieutenant smiled sarcastically, while his partner was rummaging through the kitchen. "He's going on a trip," he suddenly shouted lifting up the shopping bag and dumping it on the kitchen table. "Look, Comrade Lieutenant, have you seen college boys dressing like this," throwing pink underwear into the air.

Frank did not know if he should be embarrassed or scared. Should he demand an explanation or offer a defensive speech? He remained quiet, while he was told that the mass murderer of our fellow communist brothers, who came to our rescue, lived or at least stayed at this address, maybe even this apartment. He also announced with pride, that one Frank Bartha was under arrest by the legal authorities. Out of respect for his father, he was told, he would not be handcuffed and should be restrained only by his own will; that they would quietly walk the seven-city block distance to his father's office for further instructions. It was the utmost necessity that they avoid any spectacle on the trip for their very own safety. He was ordered to make it look like a nonchalant stroll on the sidewalk.

'What is he doing?' Erika thought covering her gasping mouth with her shaking fingers. 'Those are his father's men. Is he going home? It must be over; yes, it is over for me!'

As they carefully walked down the torn up pavement, Frank could not see the shadow of the young girl in the doorway across the street. He could not know, that the quiet tears flowing down her cheeks were for Frank Bartha whom she would never want to see again.

4

The lightweight Zetor tractor easily dragged the flatbed full of potted flowers to be stored under the temporary canopy. The young driver twisted around on the small uncomfortable seat earnestly trying to navigate backing up to the makeshift shelves of timber and cement blocks. A small group of local high school girls was busy with arranging an earlier load of colorful plants that would decorate the Agriculture Expo that would open tomorrow.

The flatbed moved slowly to the site. The girls watched expectantly. The driver watched the girls. The inevitable collision slightly moved that crucial cement block which, in turn toppled five rows of shelving, hurling dozens of chrysanthemums and geraniums towards and on top of the screaming, falling young helpers. The Zetor abruptly stopped and the driver jumped off to aid the girls.

"You stupid blind idiot," one screamed, "you drive this for a living?"

"I'm sorry, I'm sorry," the kid apologized earnestly.

"I didn't think I was that close. Are you all right?"

"I am buried alive, dirt and flowers on top of me, you think I am all right?" one blurted, scrambling to stand up.

Those uninvolved in the accident were already helping their pals; nothing seemed to be serious, except for the broken pots and dislocated flowers.

The driver reached down to rescue the last girl from the debris. "I'm only a college student. I don't normally drive these things," he began to explain.

"You certainly proved that point," the girl said rearranging her clothing. "I hope your education is more progressive than your driving ability."

"Anything I can do?"

"Yeah, get lost!"

But anger was already missing from her tone of voice, and the handsome young man was now more of an attraction than a nuisance. The gang began to clean up the mess before authorities could make an issue of the damage.

The great Agriculture Expo of 1956 was one of the first public displays and testimonies that socialist Hungary was still the Bread Basket, not to all of Europe, but at least to most of the fledging communist world. Scheduled for early September, the affair was planned, declared and expected to be the greatest. Hundreds of collective farms were enticed to participate by showing their best, while state farms were instructed to prove the effectiveness of central planning and control. Tons of produce, flowers and other landscape decorations were hauled to the capital to amaze city folks with the creativity of Hungarian peasantry. Hundreds of exquisite breeds of animals were scheduled to be placed on display, and offered up for an exchange of ownership. Herds of beautiful horses, very large pigs, and overproducing hens were corralled for the crowds to view. Demonstrations of milking cows with the latest equipment, competition style fleecing of sheep, even the lawless training of sheepdogs' herding prowess were scheduled to amuse the expected myriads of visitors.

Hungary had always been considered a great food producer in Central Europe. Its feudalist form of government for the past several hundred years extolled the power of very large farms of aristocrats, as well as the usefulness of the countless small lot peasants' fertile lands to feed the country's almost eight million population. Then a big change occurred at the end of World War II. Hungary, on the losing side of the conflict, was sanctioned to be under the occupation of the great Soviet Union. Thousands of troops in strange uniforms roamed the countryside while political forces edged out the very segmented groups of opposition to help the communists win the predestined, but first "democratic" election in 1948.

A system of Socialism was installed to demonstrate that Communism could produce a victorious, desirable lifestyle. Properties, everything from factories to private homes were 'nationalized', churches were closed, and the millions of acres of fertile land were divided into large State Farms and small parcels of individual garden-farms. Anyone who owned a hoe and proved to be of peasant ancestry was presented with some land to call his own. People toiled their dirt earnestly until they realized that one hoe would not sufficiently cultivate five to ten acres of land, not even good land at that.

The new government rushed to the rescue. The new small farmers were told that if their land would be combined into large and feasible parcels, the State Farms would loan them tractors and heavy cultivating equipment to work their farms. Thus, the copycat of the Soviet Kolhoz system, the Collective Farm was finagled into the ideal form of Agriculture in Hungary. By 1956 hardly any land was in private use.

"I'm Frank Bartha," the driver college student said as he wiped off his hand on the side of his trousers before extending it for a handshake.

"Erika Molnar, a sophomore at Arpad High School," she returned the courtesy. "What do you study?"

"Not driving tractors for sure. Political Science, if that would please you better."

"Stay off that contraption before you kill someone. You Political Scientist, you."

In the meantime, the flatbed was unloaded; the driver from a nursery farm returned and the task of beautifying the Expo was getting into proper order. Slowly, as the sun took its regular turn over the Danube River, student volunteers began to gather at their designated bus stops. Frank nonchalantly kept pace with Erika.

"Ready to go?"

"Got to feed my grandfather, why?"

"Just asking," he said like it was not important.

"Where are you going?" not even looking at him.

"Oh, I don't know. Maybe to the movies, or something."

"I guess you aren't tired either. What movie?"

"What do you like? Have you seen 'She danced only One summer' with Ulna Jacobson? It's Swedish with Hungarian subtitles."

"I heard it's very good."

"It is, I've seen it a dozen times."

"You pay to see a movie a dozen times?" She looked at him suspiciously.

"Of course not. I have a part time job in a projection room."

She got interested now in the projection room, high above all the spectators, where all that magic on a piece of white canvas was created. "I guess it is not possible to show that place to me," she finally said expecting disappointment.

"I can do anything I want," he said, "whatever you would like."

The bus just pulled up and the crowd of students pressed on. Frank moved right behind her placing both hands on her shoulders so as not to be separated. She didn't seem to mind. As they reached the center isle of the double unit bus she turned with her back against the wall. She suddenly realized that she was between his arms, face to face, almost touching. She did not know how to move. He looked deeply into those hazel eyes that had fascinated him the most about this girl. He slowly let one arm down and politely placed his palm on the wall behind her. He blushed for the first time.

Two more transfers to different streetcars and almost an hour later they were on a side street facing the movie house.

"I must call my grandfather about this," she said, almost apologetic that she wasn't old enough to control her own life. Without any discussion she stepped into the first phone booth. A few minutes later she pushed the folding door open. "How long is this movie?"

Frank pulled up his shoulders. "Pretty long, I guess."

"I must be home by ten," she said when she joined him again.

"Great. Ten it is." He automatically reached for her hand. They proceeded to the service door and he searched his pockets for the key.

The feature movie, according to the customs of the time, was presented continuously from ten in the morning until midnight. If a film was especially well liked, tickets to each show were sold out sometimes for days in advance, and the same program was presented sometimes for months.

Seeing this promising movie on a whim made Erika feel like somebody special. Frank led her up the narrow, steep steps to the projection room. With the soundtrack hardly audible, they could still hear the Clarinet Polka flowing in to embrace them. They put their heads close to the small service window, their faces touching, he still holding her hand. The dancing young couple on the canvas seemed an astonishing resemblance, and even the tragic end of the story could not break the magical feeling of their fledging relationship.

But all the other movies they enjoyed together, the quiet strolls in the city park, and visits to art museums could not break the magic of the Clarinet Polka. For Erika Molnar and Frank Bartha swaying in what they felt was their music, holding hands, gazing into each other's eyes, it was a special world, just for them; even if they did not kiss until a month later, following the customs of young lovers of that time.

*   *   *

Now, as Frank was quietly escorted by the AVO to receive his deserved reprimand, he thought of the long warm afternoons, the sweet smell of her hair, the burning press of her lips. He also felt the heavy guilt of his failed mission, the painful worry over their future together. He could not believe anything worse could follow. He just walked between his captors, his bowed head heavy with discontent. The other side of the AVO that he had never seen waited for him in the building they were approaching.

Captain Bartha was a Political Officer of the AVO, the Hungarian equivalent of the Russian KGB. His plush office was on the second floor of its Headquarters, an impressive townhouse nestled among a higher class of residences of Old Pest. It had originally been built around the turn of the century for a Jewish industrialist family who were deposed, deported and eventually perished during the Nazi campaign in 1944. For a short time the four story home became headquarters for the new Hungarian Nazi Party. At the end of the war, looting depleted most of the fancy furnishings; then the Russian Army lodged some of their officers there, thus saving the paneled walls and hardwood floors from the normally destructive behavior of their common infantrymen.

The communists promoted Comrade Bartha to a high position in 1948 when their party gained political power to control the country. During the war he was a POW in Russia, a foot soldier from a poor peasant family, a perfect candidate to be pulled out of the prison camp and properly indoctrinated to the service of world communism. Today, he faced his most difficult task as a Party leader. His son was ushered into his office.

"Normally, we just shoot traitors who betray our country. Normally, we don't even ask questions," the Captain announced quietly, slowly rising from behind his desk. "But damn it, this is not a normal circumstance!" he shouted into his son's face. Then he turned to his underlings. "You are excused."

"Let me tell you what I know," he continued when they were alone. "You were found in the company of murderers and enemies of our homeland. You escaped custody and were later found breaking into government property and in possession of material things that were not yours." The captain took a deep breath. "We are in a bloody war with misguided stupid people put up to it by foreign western powers. Our enemy wants to destroy everything we have accomplished so far in this country and kill us all in the process. Are you the enemy of the people?"

Frank lowered his eyes, like he always did in presence of his father. He just stood there motionless, not uttering a word. Visions from the past few days rolled around his head. He saw workmen in shabby clothing toppling the great statue of Joseph Stalin, and his cut off head being dragged down the main avenues of the capital. He heard the screaming and shouting of obscenities; shoving the bust of the most respected leader of the communist world into the middle of the busiest intersection of the city, and he witnessed the disgusting spitting on its face until the dark bronze turned snow white. Then the images changed to the lifeless old body of Erika's grandfather, and he felt the warm blood on his face when the AVO shot that unknown innocent woman. The visions were swirling around with the slogans that were drummed into his consciousness by years of communist schooling. And the chaos became a nightmare chasing him through this confusing world until it stopped in front of the skinny girl whom he now not only cherished but also began to adore. No, more than that, his feelings for Erika became an unconditional love. He suddenly felt a longing and belonging to the tiny world that was only his and hers. He realized again, looking up to his father's angry face, that it was so remarkably obvious now that they were, father and son, looking at life from opposite directions.

"I was visiting a friend, a girl friend, that is all."

"You are the product of our chosen beliefs. You were raised and educated by the generosity of the great powers you are cowardly trying to deny. In the middle of our most important struggle for existence you are shamefully following your animal instincts? Is that the gratitude your country deserves?"

"I am grateful for being alive," Frank said a little louder, "I am also grateful that my mother will never know all this. I am sorry that you feel ashamed of me, but the product you are talking about is a growing, developing intellect beginning to see more clearly by the flares of this war. Now you may introduce me to the forces for blind obedience." Frank said quietly as he lifted his clinched hands and crossed them with stubborn resistance.

"You deserve this," his father shouted and opened the office door. "Lieutenant, get him out of my sight!"

* * *

The basement of the building was not much different from any ordinary sub floor. In its dark corners there was a furnace and a large storage bin for coal. Another storage area became visible as Frank was escorted, now with brutal force, towards the far end of the building. Armed guards opened a large steel door into a lighted long white corridor. Frank knew that now they were long past the building's periphery, and they must be somewhere under the street. At the end of this underground passageway they went into a tee, where steel bars were closing a row of small cubicles jammed full with people.

There must have been hundreds of prisoners here, political prisoners, he supposed, since the AVO never got involved with common criminals, only with intellectual enemies of the state. There was hardly any space on the floors to sit down, and if there were any sanitary provisions, he could not see them. After a long walk, one of his guards produced some keys and he was shoved into a seemingly full cubicle.

The place was relatively quiet. The enemies of the state were mostly educated people who did not agree with the political views of the reigning regime; religious leaders who did not accept atheism as the new doctrine of the country; and small farmers who did not willingly give up their land and homes to cooperative agriculture. Frank knew very well who these people were; it was part of the Political Science curriculum at college. What he could not fathom was why these people were here in an otherwise unknown location, and not at one of the publicized criminal detention camps. He sensed the hush of his cellmates as he was pushed amongst them.

A burly man, the nearest to him, spoke up. "You are too young to be a priest, too skinny to be a farmer, and too clean to be an unemployed actor," he analyzed the new prisoner. "You must be a spy!"

Frank did not know what to say. He could not tell them that he was the son of their chief warden, that he was a junior at the best political science university of Eastern Europe. None of that would help him to survive in this rat hole or gain acceptance. He plainly must tell them the other truths that could benefit him.

"They think I have killed an AVO officer."

"If you did, they would have shot you right there," the burly one said, "You just want our sympathy."

"It is the truth," Frank protested. "There are many casualties of the revolution."

"What revolution?" The crowd begun to murmur in nervous disbelief.

They surrounded him with gaping faces as he slowly recalled the events of the past few days; the long march of the largest crowd since the last government ordered May Day parade; how the peaceful demonstration became the political cry of the people: "Russians Go Home!" And how this dissent spread throughout the capital and by nightfall Stalin was no more a respected leader. Frank also told them about the first gunfire at the radio station and the consequent battles between the AVO and the general public; how the youth of the Universities, and even high schools, fought the incoming Russian tanks with Molotov cocktails; how some of the Hungarian military joined the uprising; the general strike that numbed the city to a standstill, and how Erika revenged her grandfather's death.

His story was greeted with quiet attention to every word. The spark of freedom began to show in their eyes, and questions popped up even from the adjoining rooms within earshot. "Why are we still here?"

The force that held them captive lay behind one single steel door. And help from the freedom fighters could not come, simply because the location of this prison was unknown to the outside world. But the revolution already uncovered many other deceptive communist institutions hidden throughout the country; an ammunition factory under a plant producing chocolate; a center to listen into every telephone conversation in the city located in a cave in Buda; and a spy training facility under a girl's dormitory. But at this moment, no one in the capital knew about the existence of the 487 political prisoners under one of the busiest streets in the city. And then, small puffs of smoke began to flow in from the air ducts above their jail.

* * *

The bookstore on Lenin Boulevard was appropriately named KNIGA, or BOOK in Russian. It sold only copies of literature in Russian language, by Russian authors, mostly political works of course, and it was widely known only as the Russian Book Store. By Saturday night, the fourth day of the revolution, dissatisfaction and anger concentrated on the mere presence of Russian troops on Hungarian soil. Out of the twelve-point list of demands what the freedom fighters wanted most was to get all the Russians and their communist puppets out of the country. With that, anything connected to the unwanted occupation also had to go.

It was almost an act of heroism to break down the doors to the bookstore, ravish its shelves of all that propaganda, pile it on the pavement in front, and set it on fire. The consequent bonfire reached the power lines of the streetcars above. The destruction was augmented with kerosene, and any liquid that would accelerate the fire. No one paid any attention to the burning fluid seeping into the storm sewers that was slowly spreading to the underground. Not until, that is, the sounds of screaming cries for help overpowered the shriveling crackle from the burning of the hated words of Lenin and Stalin.

Curiosity turned into astonishment, then to quick action. The fire was diverted from the manholes and water subdued the flames. Heavy construction equipment was brought in and the digging began. Sanitation experts showed up to evaluate the situation, and fighters with red-white-green armbands broke down the doors to the Central Office for Adult Education and found the political prisoners under the now desolate, unguarded building. Frank Bartha was among those rescued.

5

The old cobblestones separated easily and the machine stopped and restarted to follow the faint cries of "Down here, down here." The rescuers, a small brigade from the Ironworks of Csepel, came quickly with heavy equipment when the word got out that another secret political prison had been discovered. When the ceiling of one of the underground cells finally broke through, strong arms began to pull out and fill the street with dazed, ragged skeleton like figures, men in shabby clothing, pale, desperately trying to avoid sunlight. Other Freedom Fighters eager to help smashed in the front door of the nearest building, the School for Adult Education. Unbelievably, they encountered no resistance, nor objections. The halls were empty and locating the entrance to the underground seemed easy.

"Stop the digging! Stop the digging!" a young man shouted running up to the machine. "We found the door, we are in!"

The prisoners came through the debris of glass now, holding onto the swinging large door, not hurrying, accepting their rescue, still in a daze. By the time the dreaded place was emptied, and searching for the feeble and sick concluded, the sun was dropping behind the hills of Buda. A small truck arrived with some food and water. Familiar faces greeted each other enthusiastically, for even if they had been confined here for months or years, they couldn't tell if their friends or relatives had shared their sufferings. Some, who lived in the capital, began their slow march to their homes on foot. The others waited for their accustomed instruction on what to do next.

No one there knew what to do next. They were free to go, too weak to be expected to join the fight, too anxious to find their families. The ironworkers from Csepel got back on their truck, leaving the government's equipment where it stopped. Abandoning communist government property seemed to be part of fighting for freedom.

Frank first thought to go home after all. The affluent residential section of Rozsadomb in Buda where the Bartha family lived was quite a long way on foot, but he felt strong after his short imprisonment, empowered by anger and an urge to straighten things out with his father.

Margit Bridge, the obvious and only route home, still picked up some bright glare from the Danube. A group of ex-prisoners, several hundred of them, spread out on the pavement of the empty boulevard. It was too late to notice that two Russian tanks blocked the road to the bridge; it was too late to avoid the spraying bullets coming from both sides of the avenue. Hitting the ground instinctively saved many lives. The ones who survived the brief attack were quickly transported into the waiting open-bed trucks.

The bridge hurriedly was opened for the military convoy speeding down on Martirok Boulevard, zooming by the statue of General Bem, the Polish hero of over a hundred years ago, the one who inspired this uprising in the first place. The leading commander in the armored car headed straight to the major railway center at Kelenfold. A large crew of servicemen stood there, and it did not take long to shave everyone's head, strip and garb them in *gimnastorkas*, the Russian khaki military shirt, long sleeved and hanging loose to mid thigh. Its customary belt was not provisioned for safety reasons, nor were they given hats to cover their now bright domes.

Frank had no ability to stop them, only to protest heartily in the language that he had been forced to learn since fifth grade.

"I am innocent. I do not belong to this mob," he kept saying, but the Russian ears seemed not to understand his dialect. He was simply shoved over to get dressed, clumps of his hair sticking to his now shivering body. Dressing like a Russian seemed to be a better alternative than freezing.

A soldier in officer's uniform strolled by uninterested. Frank jumped in front of him crying. "I am a communist," he declared. "My father is an officer of the AVO!" The man in charge understood clearly the predicament of the shivering skinny figure he looked upon in contempt.

"You are a traitor then!" he shouted in perfect Hungarian. His left hand clenched in a fist, he laid out the first punch. Frank's face twisted in pain, his affected eye shut in defense, but he stood his ground. Only the next blow made him roll over exposing his back to receive a direct hit to his kidney. He collapsed in agony, not feeling the sharp boot in his groin, not hearing the muzzled sounds of his breaking ribcage.

"Get this dirty pig out of here before I kill him," the officer screamed in disgust. Frank's limp, unconscious body lay in a bundle on the ground before he was dragged into a boxcar and dropped in the middle of the entrance. As the other prisoners were instructed to get on the train, one by one they stepped over him, unsure of what to do. Try to provide some aid, or to finish the job? To this group of political prisoners, Frank Bartha did not deserve either one. The train began to move slowly. No one even bothered to close up the boxcar.

At first, it was unimportant which way the train was headed. Most probably to a concentration camp in the Soviet Union, they all guessed, but on the other hand, the communists had enough immediate problems of their own without getting involved with more troublemakers. The small crew of prison guards was not even surprised when their route was intercepted by a disabled streetcar at the next intersection. They all jumped off the slow moving engine as it plowed into the makeshift steel barricade. When the train finally came to a halt, there was no one there to meet the freed again prisoners, nor to shoot the escaping Russian soldiers. The intersection was now totally blocked to movement in any direction.

When Frank awoke to a painful consciousness in the total darkness, he wasn't sure he was alive, and yet, his logic told him that it would be senseless to believe in another world if pain accompanied you there. And the pain was surely there, and it did not make any difference in this world if he was a communist or a revolutionary; he just wanted to die. He was still in the middle of the boxcar, alone in his agony.

He realized that if he opened his eyes all the way, there would be some light sifting in through the open door. Slightly turning his aching head, he noticed the endless rows of tracks emitting a dull glimmer across the rail yard. Occasionally distant gunfire rattled, others returned the fire indicating that the revolution was still in progress. He made a small fruitless move to get to a sitting position.

"My own comrades tried to kill me, and the freedom fighters thought me despicable. Where am I, what have I done to deserve this?" he murmured aloud to himself. He had always strived to do the right thing. If the homeland was led by a communist government, it was his patriotic duty to serve and support that government. The enemies of the state were clearly identified. Rich capitalists, who exploited the working class; the aristocracy oppressing the peasants; priests who could not swallow agnostic ideas; they were surely considered dangerous opponents of socialist thinking. Why was it so outrageously objectionable to help the poor of the world help themselves anyway? Why would some misguided people sacrifice their own lives to change the inevitable course of history by opposing their legitimate government?

But his pain reminded him of other events of the past few days; the senseless killings and destruction, his father's blind faith in his system; and then, Erika's frightened face emerged in his blurry eyes. It must be more right on her side of the world that adds up to more wrong on his. No, his world cannot be right anymore, there must be a God or some supreme being out there somewhere who would not tolerate more wrongs. If he could just muster up enough strength to move towards that world. Even if for nothing else, then for Erika's sake. He must go and find her.

It was mid morning when he regained consciousness again, but the pains were still there. He tried to move his limbs. The arms responded well, but both legs were numb, perhaps from the position he was in for so long. Hanging on to the side of the door, he slowly lowered himself to the ground. With great effort he was able to stand up. No one was around to observe as he relieved himself. His stomach was empty by now; he could not remember his last meal, but food was not important. He found a piece of a picket fence to balance on, and began to drag himself across the railroad yard. On the street that he thought would take him out of the city there was no traffic at all. The sidewalk was all his, and with one hand against the walls, the other on his stick; he seemed to gain power and speed.

Two boys approached him in the middle of the road. They had to be ten or twelve at most; one had a cigarette hanging out of the corner of his mouth, both brandished Russian made submachine guns. Their eyes roamed both sides of the street, the doorways, the balconies, and the rooftops. They seemed to be frightened. Would they take him for a Russian soldier and cut him down without a word, Frank thought in horror. Would they at least observe his feeble condition and walk on? Would they feel mercy in their young hearts?

"*Drostuthy Towarish*," one of the boys said as they stopped a few feet away.

"I don't speak Russian," Frank blurted out in a low voice, "I was a prisoner of the AVO. Are there enemies where you came from?"

"No, friend. You are safe almost to Bicske. After that, who knows?"

"Thanks," Frank said with a sigh of relief, "God be with you."

He did not know if these boys knew about God, or how far Bicske was. The empty road ahead became reassuring, this latest adrenaline surge almost made him abandon his walking stick. But it was also a weapon after all.

The buildings were lower now; one or two stories high at the most, with more empty spaces between them, more room for the small town gardener. Asters, mums and petunias colored the small strip of dirt in front of the homes; sunflowers shook their heavy bowed heads in the breeze. There was no war this far out of the city. He felt the sun was beckoning to him from the other side of the street. He felt strong enough to try to cross it. The half-ton pick up nearly hit him.

The driver stopped abruptly, and a freedom fighter jumped out from the passenger side.

"Can we take you somewhere?" asked a middle-aged man coming up to him. "Soldiers get a crew cut, only prisoners are shaven. Are you all right?"

When Frank did not say anything the man led him towards the end of the truck. Someone lowered the back gate and many arms lifted him up. He crawled into the straw pile in the middle, and the truck moved on. Slowly, Frank told the half a dozen teenagers what seemed to be a life story, from the firing squad to the Russian prison train. He did not tell about his father, or the AVO man in the rest room. In turn he was informed that the group was on a scavenging hunt for weapons; that a small garrison was only a half hour away, that he needed to be out of the *gimnastorka* and he should have a hat.

In the back of the truck a small wooden box hid some basic repair tools for the vehicle. It also contained a greasy overall the driver would use when needed. Carefully he was undressed and clothed again, his pitiful Russian garment tossed to the roadside and a small cap covered his baldness. Exhausted from the ordeal, he tried desperately to express his gratitude by making small circles in the air with an outstretched palm. He wasn't sure if he was understood, or even what he tried to say.

When the truck stopped at the front of a tavern, the boys hurriedly jumped off. The bartender was told about their mission and he gladly provided them with some slices of bread thinly smeared with lard. Because of their age, they were served bottles of Jaffa drinks, the Eastern Block's orange Kool-Aid. The three men from the driver's cab took their beer, naturally. A boy brought a slice of bread and glass of beer for Frank. The excruciating pain in his jaws fought a battle with his extreme hunger. Somehow, he managed to swallow a few bites. With the short break over, the truck rattled on towards the west.

The driver slowed down as they approached the garrison. The side road they turned into seemed to end at the large ochre colored building. One of the boys lifted up and waved a Hungarian flag, the red-white-green stripes with a large gap in the middle where the official seal of the communist government had been hacked out with a knife. The building appeared to be empty. The large double gate leading to an inner court was wide open; the yellow stucco walls glimmered in the setting sun. The driver inched towards the opening.

The first burst of fire hit the boy with the flag, both tumbling to the ground. The men in the cab ducked below the dashboard, the driver desperately twisting the steering wheel to turn the vehicle around. The artillery shell smashed through the windshield, but by the time it bored through the back of the seat the front tire of the truck reached the ditch at the side of the road. The vehicle tipped to the side and skidded against a large tree. All its occupants were strewn around the shrubbery, most motionless.

No one was able to stand up. The injured moaned, some screamed from pain. Frank was stunned from the landing. The truck lay on its side bridging the ditch, the engine still humming. When the soldiers arrived from the building the attack was over.

"These are stupid kids," one shouted. "Who ordered the fire?"

"We must clean up this mess," another declared.

A mess, a mistake, or friendly fire, the soldiers were

certain that it was the truck's fault. In the nervous aftermath, someone shut off the engine; others dragged the bloody bodies from the cab. One by one, dead or injured, they were carried into the garrison. Frank curled up hiding under the truck in the ditch. He did not move until darkness.

He had no idea where he was. Born and raised on the Great Plains region on the east side of the country, in his long nineteen years he had never ventured to the west side of the Danube. Straining his memory of eighth grade geography, he vaguely remembered the town of Bicske, more from history class on something tragic or heroic happening in that area during World War II, somebody blowing up a railroad bridge while a German troop train was crossing it. Or was it somewhere else? He knew he must find the tracks, a railroad station maybe, but definitely a train.

The road appeared to be a main route; a village or something must appear soon. He looked like a dirty mechanic, but how could he manage to cross half of the country with his familiar name? He wouldn't change it of course, but what if he was asked? He carried no sort of identification, the Russians made sure of that, but the name Bartha was mentioned in the media a lot, and if the revolution was winning, it would not be an asset. He must call himself somebody else.

"Barna!" he shouted with relief. "It sounds close enough, it is a fairly common surname, and what is it, only a color, and brown is a common color too." He repeated his new name a few times. It began to sound familiar. 'Now, where is Bicske?' he wondered.

6

Erika met Tessa at the farmers market. Tessa was about Erika's age, a sophomore in a technical school, and worked at the market on weekends to help her family. She was a Schwab, a descendant of German people who settled in Hungary many generations ago, who stubbornly held on to their customs, language and traditions. Often, resentments flared up between the Schwabs and the Magyars in the olden days, but by now, most neighborhoods had learned to live in peace, just residing on two different sides of the street, at least in the villages. In the cities the melding was much easier, and members of minorities could even become friends with Hungarians.

Tessa's family, the Khuns, were farming in the Aprofalu area, a small village just north of the capital, on the fertile banks of the Danube River. They grew vegetables and some fruits, and with the clever storage techniques of the time, were able to keep a stream of produce coming to the market most of the year.

The big market at Tolbukin Square was a huge steel and glass building where, on several floors, hundreds of small farmers, butchers and grocers had their little stands and cubicles, where they peddled their products.

Erika turned out to be a regular at the Kuhn's stand, and the two girls became sort of weekend friends, without getting their families involved, or visiting each other's residences. Each time they met, they learned a bit more about each other, and Erika even met two of Tessa's sisters and a brother. Now Tessa was the only living person outside of the capital to whom she could turn to.

Erika was born in Budapest, and had lived all her fifteen years in the city. She knew her way around even in remote areas; she knew where all the streetcars went, under what number, and on what route. Now it was easy for her to walk through the city, able to sneak across major avenues and avoid areas of fighting. She went around Hero's Square, although it was quiet there now, but she did not want to take any chances. Sprawling municipalities ringed the capital; heavy industry, huge mills and factories of all kinds were supported by thousands of workers living within walking distance of their workplace in huge 'cement towers' of government dwellings. She walked past industrial buildings, idle from the general strike. Men in small groups guarding the closed gates paid little attention to the girl from the city.

By midnight, cold and very tired, Erika reached the part of the village with single-family houses and little gardens, the area where the Kuhns might be living. This was all foreign territory to her, and there were no streetlights to guide her. The village rested quietly in darkness.

Finally Erika saw a small light shining through a window facing the sleeping street. Sneaking over, she peered into the room and saw a young woman, dressed in a long flannel nightshirt, bending over a crib. She could not see clearly, but she supposed there was a baby in it. All of a sudden the long hard day got to her. Her stiff fingers barely touching the windowpane made some scratching sounds to get the woman's attention. She knew she must make a louder noise, but there was no more strength left in her to do it. She slowly collapsed against the low windowsill.

When she came to she was lying on a straw mattress in a kitchen. The crude wooden box that served as a bed was warm, and an old man, who must have slept in there earlier, was standing next to the young woman at the foot of the bed. Erika opened her eyes then swallowed the cold liquid that was forced into her mouth. The homemade palinka, a popular Hungarian brandy, burned all the way down. She began to gag and jerked into a sitting position.

"Go, drink it," the old man said, "It will help."

She fought off the cough and tears burned her eyes. The palinka began to warm her stiff body and she forced down a couple more sips.

"There, there. You'll be all right," the young woman said, "Are you hungry?"

She nodded, she thought, and let herself fall back on the cot. The woman asked the old man to make a fire in the stove, and turned to take Erika's shoes off. It was chilly in the kitchen and the woman brought out an old housecoat. Then the baby cried out and she left the room.

"How is the city?" the old man asked. "Are we winning?"

'Who's we?' she thought, and then she glanced at the small crucifix on the wall. She knew she was at a safe place.

"It's quiet now," she finally said, "But the Russians are everywhere,"

"The bastards!" the old man blurted.

The kindling in the stove caught on fast and flames flashed through the side of the cast iron door. The crackling and the hint of smell of wood smoke made her feel already warmer. The woman came out again from the bedroom.

"All I can get you is toast and some tea," she said apologizing. "We've had no stores open for some time now. I must toast the bread; it's kind of old. Maybe a little garlic?" Erika nodded again.

The woman cut some of the rye bread and laid the slices on the not yet hot stovetop. Water was warming on the other side for tea, and she started to clean some cloves of garlic. The bread began to smoke, and she quickly turned each of them over. When both sides were done, holding with three fingers, she vigorously rubbed the garlic against the scorched sides of the bread.

"It stank up your fingers now," Erika said as she moved over to the kitchen table.

"It's all right. I've had worse." She poured some tea into a tin cup, and then added a few drops of palinka to the reddish liquid. "Where are you heading?" she asked.

"I came to visit some friends."

"Who?"

"The Kuhns, you know them?"

"Which one, the kofa?"

"Yes, the market-lady. How did you guess?"

"She's the only one who goes to the city often enough to be known by somebody."

"I know Tessa, the younger daughter."

"You must get some sleep now. The old man will take you there in the morning." She waited until Erika finished eating, and then cleared off the table. They did not put any more wood on the fire. The old man was sitting on a small stool at the end of the cot, yawning. He lit a cigarette and waited for morning.

When the sun came up, groggy from their disturbed sleep, the old man took Erika to find her friend. They found no one at home at the Kuhns.

"They went west," a middle aged woman shouted across the fence from next door. "Are you some kind of relative or something?"

"No, I don't even know them," the old man said. "This girl knows them from the market. What do you mean went west?"

"That's the Schwab for you. A bit of commotion, and off they go, back to Germany. My John always said they should get rid of them. Now, some are leaving on their own."

"Shut your big mouth and let them be," a deep male voice came from the other house. The woman turned around without another word and disappeared.

"How can you just cross the border like that?" Erika asked. She knew that not even all the communists could get a passport to go to a western country, at least not without a great deal of hassle, and not the whole family all at once.

"I don't know anybody who has gone west from here," the old man said, "But we never had a revolution before either."

Erika thanked the old man again, and turned towards the main road.

"Are you sure you're gonna be all right?" the old man asked with concern.

"Sure," she said. "I'm the only one I have to take care of."

The country road out of Aprofalu was quiet in the early morning hours. Not that later in the day there would be more travelers going this way. Only local farmers used this hard packed bitumen to and from their fields, but it was already November, most of the harvesting was done and it was not quite time for the fall plowing. The fighting of the revolution had begun to spread to the countryside too. Villagers banned together, searching for weapons and trying their best to get rid of anything that related to the Russians and definitely to communism. Those who stayed on the side as spectators of the conflict did it from behind curtained windows, nervously waiting for the outcome. The news that Russian tanks had flooded the streets of Budapest had not yet reached this region.

The sun on its daily trip to bring another pleasant, unseasonably warm day with no rain in sight. Erika almost enjoyed the walk, following the narrow path that bicycles and pedestrians had worn all summer along the side of the road. No grass grew on this path, laid out like a carelessly thrown ribbon curving in regular intervals around utility poles. Her thin coat gave some comfort, and aside from the short, restless night, she felt a little better and ready to assess her life and plan her future, if there was one. Politics and fighting had no rationality in her young mind, only thoughts of nourishment, more rest, and where to get all that. She didn't know how far the next village could be, or how far her tired legs could take her. She only knew that better circumstances would come and somehow, she would survive all this.

She had plenty of time to think of Frank, the good, passionate and friendly Frank. She desperately tried to block out her last vision of him, the walking away from her apartment with his friends, for she was sure that's who they were. And they were sure that Erika Molnar was the one they should be looking for, and there was a well-informed Frank Bartha who would lead them on her trail. She could hardly believe that the AVO was not after her by now.

Suddenly, a noise behind her interrupted her angry thoughts.

The clip-clop of a single horse on the blacktop behind her made her turn. Pulling a small wagon half full of hay, the fast approaching animal blew hot steam through its nose; a long and fast drive must have caused its exhaustion. A lone man in his thirties held the reins in one hand, and a small whip in the other. As he caught up with Erika he slowed to her pace.

"Going far, my Doll?"

Erika stopped and looked up to the man on the wagon. He was a typical farmhand, dark pants, canvas coat, his light shirt buttoned to the top, his dark mustache hanging over a friendly smile.

"Can I give you a lift somewhere?" the stranger asked on also stopping.

She bowed quietly, slowly losing her strength.

"Hop on then, Janos will not harm young girls on the country road."

Erika wondered why country people generally assume strange girls to be their close friends, but on the other hand, why would formality make any difference today. She took the seat next to him for a much needed rest.

"Erika," she offered her hand as a brief introduction.

"Delighted," he said in return.

Was there anything else to say? She surely wouldn't tell this man that she was planning to leave the country, and why. The horse seemed to enjoy the short rest, and began strolling without any encouragement from the driver.

"You don't have many animals, do you?" she asked, just to start a conversation.

"No, not many. Why do you ask?"

"For the small load of hay you carry. Seems not worth the trip."

Janos glanced back to his load nervously. Did his cargo look suspicious in this revolutionary turbulence? Did he pick up someone of the wrong side? Would his generosity bring unwanted consequences? No, he thought, she is too young and gentle looking.

"Are all city girls so knowledgeable about how much hay animals need?"

"No, just asking." She felt sorry that she started this.

"Good," Janos smiled. "So, what's up in the big city, because you are not from this area for sure.

"I wouldn't know, I left some time ago."

"And no luggage, no winter coat? My Doll, you are running away from home!"

"I have no home," she said bluntly.

"I'm so sorry," Janos said with all honesty. "I'll take you to our village anyway."

"Thank you. You are generous."

The horse turned the bend on the road with familiarity.

"What now?" Janos cried out. Just beyond the bend, at the crossroad, an army jeep became visible. The unit seemed to be an inspection station with three infantrymen, armed with submachine guns, smoking and yakking away with no care in the world. Janos slowed down the horse to give himself time to think on the next two hundred meters they had to reach the post.

In desperation, he slowly put his arm around Erika's shoulder, and pulling the girl closer, he pushed her face into his chest.

"Hug me with both hands," he murmured.

"What?" she gasped in protest.

"Shut up! Just do it!"

She twisted her face towards the soldiers. They were Hungarians, not much of a threat on this lonely road. Not like the Russian devils not long ago. He pressed her face back with more force.

The horse clip-clopped slowly, closer and closer. Janos bowed down and kissed the top of Erika's head again and again. Then he picked up her face and pressed his lips on her mouth. The soldiers got closer and closer, their threatening silence slowly turned to small giggles. The horse snorted and swung both of his front legs in the air, narrowly missing a young girl on a bicycle.

"Wow. Long live the counter-revolution!" a soldier exclaimed.

"Shut up, you fool," another says, "They are getting ready for their honeymoon."

Clippety-clop, the horse passed the jeep. The startled girl jumped off her bike and grabbed the large bag of red apples off the handlebar. The soldiers' attention shifted in her direction. Janos squeezed the handle of the whip and let go of Erika.

"You need more enticement old man," a soldier shouted. "How you going to handle a young chick like that?" He smirked as he pulled out his handgun. The crack of the single shot reverberated in the warm air. The horse jumped on all fours into a frightened gallop. Roaring laughter followed them from behind.

The whip unnecessarily struck the horse's back; Janos realized he was still alive. Erika moved to the far end of their narrow seat. She turned to the side, away from him, quietly shaking off the tears from her cheeks. She sensed their ordeal was over.

"You dirty pig!" she cried.

"I saved our lives," he said straightening up and calming the horse at the same time.

"I didn't need to be saved from anything," she lied.

"You are a freedom fighter," he said turning towards her. "I smelled gasoline and gunpowder on your hair. You are running from a fight."

"What about you then?" she cried without admitting anything.

"You don't smell of gunpowder!"

"Not yet," he said and swung towards the back of the wagon. With the tip of the whip he lifted a corner of the small load of hay. At the bottom the ends of about a dozen Russian rifles were revealed. "Not yet," he repeated.

The end of the village came into view. "Sorry," Janos said, "I could not come up with a better idea. I panicked and hoped it would work. I wish you would go now," he said. "Our home is not far from here, and I don't want my wife to see us. She wouldn't understand; I hope you do."

The wagon stopped and Erika got off. "How far to the railroad station?"

"Not far," he said, "just behind those pine trees. God be with you."

She picked up speed as she passed the horse. It shook its head snorting. 'Am I supposed to be ashamed in front of you too?' she thought, 'Am I a whore now?"

The waiting room at the station was surprisingly full, farm workers with very little luggage, couples and small families, but mostly young people. The gloomy crowd made only whispering small talk one on one, mainly uncalled for explanations of their destinations. But no one would ever mention that the train they were all waiting for, if it ever comes, is heading for Tatabanya, a transfer station for the main tracks towards the western border.

She did not know anyone; she had no explanation to make. Apparently this many people would wait for only an existing transportation, no matter when it got here. But first, she must find a washroom to clean off the shame, the price she had to pay to stay alive. She forgave the stranger already, but the guilt, she knew, she would carry for some time.

Back in the waiting room she was searching for a spot at a wall, where she could, as always, slide to the floor and rest. It was close to noon, but there were no food services open anywhere, even if she had any money to buy some. The station's bar was open and crowded. It was a sad time in Hungary now, and the flow of spirits and beer made the old saying, "We Merry With Tears," more applicable than ever. The room full of men poured their sorrows out in off key, sad songs, louder than necessary, but no one worried about it.

Erika dozed off, it seemed only for a minute, but when she awoke, the sun shone through the dirty windows straight from the west. People fatigued from the long idle waiting filled all the available seats, rested on each other's shoulders, or sat on floors and waited; just waited. The ticket office was empty; only a small, hand written note informed the travelers to pay the conductors on the train. It was a common practice in small rural areas of the country.

Suddenly the crowd was pushing toward the exits, long before the whistle of the approaching locomotive could be heard. The platform next to the tracks filled up swiftly, people shouting for lost members of their groups, hanging on to their small bundles of possessions. As the train pulled in, some grabbed the steps' railings before the cars fully stopped. It would be a small miracle if all these people would fit into the already crowded coaches. But Hungarians, under communism, were accustomed to such inconveniences.

7

'Push and shove, push and squeeze,' Erika urged herself as she maneuvered through the door of the crowded train. Slowly, the myriad of passengers began to rearrange themselves in the interior of the coaches. Some moved over to make at least a half seat for someone, others stepped in between the knees of other travelers as the benches facing each other seemed to have some empty space. Before the train lurched forward again, all the cars' capacity, and not the legal one at that, was filled to the hilt.

She tried to lean against the nearest wall space. There was no luggage to care for, no need to worry about her next meal, or how she would pay for all this. The conductor for this section was probably stuck in the middle of another coach. Neither the disintegrating government, nor its employees were at all concerned about train fares in the closing, apparently winning phase of the revolution.

The already wintry sky of the first days of November threatened another snowfall. Less than an inch covered the farmland as the train labored towards the west. The engineer knew better than to stop at any more stations. Instead he zoomed through, not even slowing down, ignoring the stationmasters' salutes and uncertain waves. It was an unusual time for such a tumult on Hungary's rail system.

The quiet conversations that began between total strangers indicated that most of the passengers had very legitimate reasons to be on this train; a wedding to attend, or visiting a sick relative were common reasons, even though, going to a 'butchery' in the country was lauded more and more often. This was the beginning of such a season, where small households in the villages slaughtered the hog they had invested all year in raising. At these all-day affairs, it took a lot of work to process a large animal to use for the rest of the year, but it was also a lot of fun, a camaraderie eagerly frequented by urban relatives. Erika did not specify, nor was she motivated to communicate her destination to anyone.

Why would she let anyone know when she wasn't sure herself? She knew very well why she was running away, but to where was still a mystery. She had rarely traveled outside the capital, had no relations living in the country, and did not know a soul on this train. If only Frank were be here. But she knew, deep in her heart, that Frank had abandoned her, and had returned to his own world where the AVO, the communist government and mostly his father demanded his allegiance. Why would a brief courtship full of foolish expectations sever such strong ties? Who is Erika Molnar to influence such a severe change?

"All my friends call me Eddy. What do your friends call you?" The young man was leaning over from the opposite wall of the foyer to start a conversation.

"Erika," she said looking up.

"Ah! Erika Dear, Do whisper in my ear that you love me," the boy sang in a low voice grabbing on to the connection. "Isn't it from 'Heart to Heart' or is it the theme song of 'Loves of Summer?"

"Never heard of it," Erika admitted. She did not frequent the theater that much. She felt ashamed that school, working at the butcher shop, and lack of funds gave an impression of an unsophisticated teenager. The young man was tall, of somewhat dark complexion, about eighteen. His long sideburns reflected one of the few western influences on Hungary unopposed by the government. He must be a college kid, Erika thought, why should she let him judge her intelligence just by not knowing a song.

"I was hoping that the song is about you and me," he said smiling. "May I be your escort to wherever your destination?"

'Here we go,' she thought, 'I can't be so attractive that guys approach me like this.'

"I am sorry, but I am engaged to be married soon," she bluffed. "Can't believe my fiancée would approve it."

"Why don't we ask him? Where is he, picking up some drinks from the dining car?"

Erika bowed her head and folded her arms as a protective shield.

"I thought so. There is no such person with us here, is there? Furthermore, high school girls do not usually marry this young. Unless they are pregnant, of course."

"Go away," she said embarrassed.

But he did not move. Out of his side pocket he produced a full pack of Kossuth cigarettes, showing that he could afford a better, and handle a stronger brand. "Where are my manners?" he cleared his voice, " May I?" as he offered the smoke. Erika felt it was her turn to embarrass him. Nonchalantly, she reached for the first cigarette of her life. He came closer to offer a light, but as she began to choke, he reached out and pulled it from her lips. He took a strong drag from it and let it dangle from his mouth as he spoke. "Right again, Erika, dear. You are way too young to smoke or get married, or even get pregnant."

"Now," he bent down and lifted a paper bag from the floor. "We shall have a small lunch, or dinner or something. I managed to bring some bread, and a couple of dry, smoked sausages from my relatives in the village. It would be my pleasure to feed, protect and provide for you in any shape or form. You first."

Erika had no other choice but to take his offer. It seemed genuine and she hadn't eaten in almost twenty-four hours. Eddy waited patiently but did not eat.

"Do you know that about this time of the day in America," and he glanced at his shiny wristwatch, "it's cocktail time? They make this extraordinary drink with great effort and precision. In a special tall glass," Eddy expertly continued, "they pour a generous portion of whisky to make the drink strong; then they add some sort of flavored soda to make it weak, fill it with ice to make it cold; and throughout the whole drinking process, they hold the glass between their palms to warm it up. Oh, and they lift it with 'this is for you' and they drink it themselves. Such people are the Americans. No wonder they have a distaste for our communism."

He pulled a liter bottle of red wine from his sack and uncorking it, he offered her a drink. She gulped and tried not to make a face. "Thank you," she mumbled, "I am sorry to be a pest. I am not accustomed to being waited on hand and foot."

"Just on foot," Eddy corrected her, smiling. "I am delighted. Now, where are we heading? The road to America, or to Austria for that matter is very treacherous and of the utmost danger. You must have a guard; you must allow me to be your guard." But before he could say 'that settles it', the screeching sound of steel sliding on steel caught everyone's attention. The train skidded to a halt at an unmistakable green semaphore. In the slight bend of the track, they could see a uniformed man shouting something into the engine compartment. For several anxious minutes the silent passengers could only hear the rhythmical release of pressure from the steam engine. On both sides of the train there were dark lifeless trees anchored to the thin layer of snow on the ground. It was obvious they were out in the middle of nowhere. One by one, conductors jumped from their posts, conversing loudly in confusion, until the news was passed on that the next railway station was occupied by heavily armed Russian soldiers. Those who did not wish to meet with them should abandon the train now.

Slowly the crowd moved towards the doors. Erika stopped briefly at the top of the coach steps. As far as she could see, dark figures of people from the train moved towards the forest in unsure small steps. In the fast approaching sunset gloom, they were searching for the Austrian border, over thirty kilometers away.

'My God,' Erika thought, 'Is everyone leaving our country?' The empty coach behind her just proved it.

As she reached the ground, Eddy close behind her; she heard the murmur of the confused crowd. People were not only looking for their traveling companions, but also, as they quickly learned, were searching for local guides to lead them to the border. The guides worked this territory, it seemed, on a regular basis, asked for nothing, but were willing to accept anything valuable, such as clothing of fur or leather, jewelry, cameras and, of course, any amount of money. In Austria, they argued, Hungarian currency was absolutely worthless.

Little by little, groups of forty or fifty gathered around two or three guides, for there were plenty to go around. The guides stood waving their long staffs, the emblem of their leadership. They were young to middle aged men from nearby villages, experts in the border landscape. Most were dressed in long pants and a shirt, although the temperature was hovering around ten Celsius and had already begun to drop. Little did they know that their guides, traveling light, were prepared to carry home the rewards of their labors.

Not that it was an easy task to do. Their route to the border was through not yet worn out trails and across deeply plowed fields, shunning established roads as much as possible. Their tempo hastened as dropping temperatures began to penetrate their light clothing. Urging on their flock regularly, they led the way almost running. If nothing came in their way, they promised, they should reach the border before midnight.

Frank Bartha appeared from nowhere. He spotted Erika first, only a few feet away. When she turned, he crunched his cap in both hands, exposing his freshly shaved head. His sheepish grin could not hide the black and blue marks on his face.

"Frank!" she cried and ran to hug him. She realized that the last time she had seen him he was not running away from her. Suddenly she understood that life was going to be good again. Tears rolling down her cheeks, she kissed him everywhere she thought he wasn't hurt. He quietly submitted to her onslaught of affection. It made him very happy.

Eddy waited patiently for a while before interrupting. "Hey lovebirds, the caravan is leaving, you better get moving." He did not think for a minute that he would have a chance with Erika again. He became polite and understanding and did not ask for an introduction. Nobody else thought about it either. Their minds were somewhere far ahead in the woods, on the long, strenuous walk awaiting them, on the strong likelihood that some would never make it. There was no information either on how many border guides had survived these trips or how many perished in the ordeal. Only one thing was certain, their future, whatever it might be, loomed in the darkness of the forest ahead.

The line of escapees stretched far back from their leaders. Many carried their meager belongings in small packets and cloth bags. Not all had a chance to prepare for this passage, to make plans and arrange for all possibilities. They were on the run, not to weddings or butcheries, but to get away for their many good reasons, mostly to escape the consequences of their deeds.

What they were running toward was just as unprepared, unplanned, and mostly unknown. While Radio Free Europe promised the full support of the free western world, that world was apparently too busy with its other crisis at the Suez Canal. In addition, that free western world in most of the refugees' minds was like the communist propaganda, half-truths and a blur of hopeful speculations. Not that they couldn't somehow believe that where they were heading was better, they were more concerned about if there would be a place to lay their already tired heads, and if there would be something to eat. For no matter what lay ahead, one desperately needed life's basic things.

Erika held on tightly to Frank's hand, desperately trying to support his wobbly steps as they rushed side by side. Frank had no luggage to burden him either. Just two young souls finding each other against incredible odds. They eagerly told their own stories, back and forth; the agonizing events of their past few days, the horrific memories that would not leave their minds.

"There is something I must tell you," Frank finally said, "I changed my name."

"You did what?" Erika looked at him strangely.

"I had to, I could not face the new world with my notable name, I am Frank Barna now."

"It is not legal, it is not fair," she spoke out. "You have a family, a past. Crossing into another country cannot change that," she argued.

"I've been thinking about that, believe me. But this is safer. I don't even want to know where I came from and who I was. This is the time to change our identity for the better, to use this opportunity to hide behind our faces, the only thing we cannot change, although the Russians tried to change mine."

"I will never do that," Erika said sternly. "My family is dead. If I am ever going to find my father in America, I want to be his Erika."

"But not a Molnar," Frank blurted out. It was not his intent to destroy this young girl's image of herself. She did not have to know what was hidden above that water tank in her apartment. But she was pulling away from him now in agonizing disbelief. He had to give her support, to explain that having a different name was not her fault, that being Jewish was not going to make her a different person. He had to tell her the truth, so she could face that new world with some wisdom and courage. He watched her reaction to his story.

"But you don't understand," she cried, "I don't know how to be Jewish! I even hate Jews!"

Frank was genuinely compassionate for her. The Great War of the world not long ago moved and shaped not only bodies but also the minds of the affected people. He knew very well how he, too, was brought up to be anti-Semitic, to blame everyone's misfortune on those who, somehow, made a better life for themselves; to be envious of their accomplishments, their fortunes and their privileged knowledge. It was politically mandated in his nation to feel this way, long before the rise of Hitler. It was very sad that his choice of love had unwittingly been required to turn against herself. He also knew, that they would, they had to overcome this dilemma.

An abrupt halt in the line ahead created some confusion. Someone had collapsed on the trail, so the guides decided to call a short rest break. Many ventured into the dark of the forest to relieve themselves; others opened packages of nourishments, even bottles of wine. Life must go on, needs had to be met. In no time, the break was over and the march was on again. Soon the trees thinned out and made way for cultivated land. Large parcels seemed to be freshly plowed, and even the light snow cover disappeared. It seemed they were approaching populated areas. The guides made a sharp turn to the left, crunching the crumbling soil under their feet. The journey, though already difficult, if it was possible, began to get worse.

The moon shone dully through sparse clouds. The crowd dispersed somewhat to allow much-needed breathing space. The headlights of an approaching car appeared in the distance. An unexpected highway was in their path.

"Get down! Get down!" the guides shouted. Dark figures collapsed to the ground row by row. Only a lone figure stood there, bending his head, which made him look like a giant question mark.

"Somebody push him down," one of the guides screamed.

"He can't," a women's small voice spoke up. "He just had a surgery yesterday, his whole torso is bandaged solid. If he lies down he will never get up again," she sobbed.

The vehicle slowly came into view. Erika stretched out her arms as she landed on now softer dirt. In the light of the car her fingers dug in for support. Support from her homeland. The car passed with indifference. As she stood up with the others, she barely noticed how she transferred a tiny part of Hungary from her palms into her coat's pockets. 'I will never leave my land now, ever," she thought. In the dark of the night her tears went unnoticed.

By eleven o'clock the moon had disappeared and on the outstretched flatland the exhausted group dragged on in the uncertain darkness. The guides stopped again. After some arguing among themselves their leader spoke up.

"You probably won't believe this, but we are lost," he said nervously. "See those lights on the right, that's the nearest village, Agota. On the left," pointing with his arm, "we are not sure. It could be another village, or a state farm. Can't tell."

The crowd nervously moved around their guides. Tired and cold, they were not too happy about the change of events. "What do you suggest we do?" someone asked.

"We decided to take a chance on the left group of lights, explore the situation and then we will come back for you," the leadsman proposed.

"All of you?" one asked again.

"We believe in strength as a team."

"Not so fast," shouted the first man, who suddenly became the leader of the group. "We also believe in the strength of our team. Two of you, and only two, will make the trip. You will come back for us, without tipping off the Russians, or whatever border guards we are facing, without leading us into a trap. You understand that?"

"Otherwise," another voice spoke up, "this poor boy you are leaving with us will get it. We went through an awful lot of killing in the past few days; one more will not make any difference."

Shouts of approval came from throughout the group and the deal was made. As the two guides disappeared in the dark, the flickering dim lights were beckoning in the distance. The would be refugees settled down for a long wait.

8

It was after five in the morning when Ken took the garbage to the dumpster in the back of the building. His night shift cleaning the drugstore was over; all he had to do now was to bring in the paper from the curb. The Hartford Courant got there about this time; the rudely twined bundle of fifty copies was dropped next to the mailbox. The folks in Winsted, on the western part of Connecticut, got their world and national news every morning reading the oldest daily in the United States.

Jack Bjorkman, the young soda jerk, was already brewing the large urn of coffee, getting ready for their morning customers. Workers at Pratt & Whitney in East Hartford, thirty miles away, began their long drive from here. So did other factory workers who had to start the day quite early. When Ken Williams punched out at five thirty, his cup of coffee and powdered jelly donut waited for him at the end of the counter. He grabbed a copy of the Courant and plopped down.

The large, bold print on the front page blared the latest: RUSSIAN TANKS CRUSHING HUNGARY. Vivid pictures showed how the mighty Soviets were crumbling up cobblestone roadbeds in search of any leftover clusters of weary freedom fighters of the now suppressed revolution.

The headline story let the American people know that only little over a decade after the war of the world, a new one may be imminent.

Ken, a Korean War veteran, knew exactly what communist armies were capable of. His limp was a lifetime reminder of the price he was paying for his GI Bill education. He was the one who had convinced Jack to enroll at the University of Hartford, and got him this job on the graveyard shift. Ken lived with his mother, a cashier at the nearby IGA food store, and he needed to help her with every day expenses. She somehow survived while he was fighting on the other side of the world. The aggressively spreading communist conquerors convinced her that, near or far, they had to be stopped somehow before they reached the beaches of Long Island. She knew that her son was destined to be part of this effort.

The late spring of 1953 brought the bad news that Marine Corporal Ken Williams had been seriously wounded and was in a military hospital in Hawaii. News like that was common in those days, but Mary Williams could not afford to leave her job to visit her son so far away. The occasional phone calls he made had to suffice. He was too ill to call after his first surgery, but a few weeks later, after the second, he had good news. He said he would survive; he'd been patched up enough to be moved to the mainland, closer to home, and no body parts were missing.

Ken spent several months recuperating in Maryland, still too far for his mother to visit. By the end of August, he was out of the hospital and enrolled at Hartford University. Living at home, commuting to school and finding part time jobs had now become routine. By Christmas he no longer needed his crutches but kept carpooling with Bjorkman.

The two spent lots of hours in heated discussions in the car on the politics of war and on the war of politics. Jack, a couple of years older, and also a veteran, was bitter about the political maneuverings over the rights and wrongs of demagogues while young soldiers paid the ultimate price on both sides of the conflict. Ken gave his country a good deal of time again just over a year ago, when devastating floods in 1955 struck his beloved town and other parts of New England. Volunteering for the Red Cross gave him more education than classrooms could ever provide. When the ordeal was over, Ken was convinced that tragedies, whether caused by men or nature, could best be faced when the ones who are able to, give a helping hand. Wars and violence come from the lowest levels of our animal instincts, he believed, and should be shunned at all costs. His devotion to help mankind obsessed his young pacifist mind.

News of the Hungarian Revolution was pouring in through all media. Radio stations provided regular updates and pictures were on the cover of every weekly magazine around the world. America was well informed from the first day on, but the Russian invasion came as a shock. The free western world extended moral support to the tiny country that dared to stand up to the communist giant; they gathered humanitarian supplies of food and medicine, but military intervention seemed out of the question. What law-abiding government would cross over neutral territory like Austria, or attack a so-called "democratic republic" nation of East Germany to get into the scuffle? Isolated on all sides, Hungary could only be encouraged and supported within the bounds of international law. Almost from the very first day of the uprising, Red Cross groups, from near and far, were gathering on the Austrian border.

Ken had to let his mother know of the new developments right away. After all, there was some Hungarian blood flowing in the Williams' veins. Grandma came to America at the turn of the century from Austria-Hungary and married an American born Slovak. Mary closed the circle by falling in love with Ken's Yankee father. Ken Williams had enough Hungarian blood to make his head swell.

"I have to call the Red Cross, they need me," he said after his mother read the news story.

"What about your studies? Your tuition is already paid and you worked hard for that money."

"This is big Mother, really big. Those people need our help."

"Let the Super Powers take care of it," she said trying not to start an argument, for it often came to a loud exchange of words when the unionized supermarket cashier and her Social Science student son engaged in solving the world's problems.

"It is just that," Ken came back, "a Super Power is whipping the butts of defenseless people. Who do you think will save them? The British are deeply involved at the Suez Canal, and we are busy electing a President. Those poor bastards over there need our help. Not the Government's, but ours, the people. They need food, shelter and medicine; like always, like every time something like this happens. Mother, I am going." He started to reach for the phone when he realized that it was too early in the day to call anyone.

"You better rest before your class starts," she said closing the discussion. She knew her son was right. It would be up to the power of the masses to deal with this. She knew that Ken Williams was a born humanitarian, and she was very proud of that.

Ken skipped his class entirely and went straight to the Registrar's Office. The events from Europe affected everyday life on campus. It was no problem to postpone his education, he was told, and if the Red Cross wanted him, that's just great. And the Red Cross surely wanted him.

His gray-blue uniform was ready by the time he arrived at the Hartford Regional Office. Many of his old friends from the flood rescue work were also there for the briefing on what to expect and what to do in Austria when they got there. A plan was formulated on the collection, shipping and distribution of basic supplies that disaster victims would need. It was planned to get all the materials and the supporting personnel straight into the war torn Hungary, but news of large groups of people actually defecting into Austria called for major additions. Now shelters had to be acquired, sanitary supplies, bedding and clothing were suddenly needed; so was the cooperation of the many organizations from the many countries that jumped into this humanitarian effort, one of the largest since World War II.

While the Austrian Government scurried for lodgings, very basic German and Hungarian dictionaries were distributed, and great efforts were made to recruit volunteers who could speak those tongues somewhat. An Operations Headquarters was thrown together in Vienna just when the first groups of refugees arrived. It was there that Ken Williams learned that the Russian Army had fortified and actively closed down the Hungarian border in both directions. It took only a few days for the stunted freedom fighters to outmaneuver the soviet military might and begin trickling into Austria's neutral territory again. They came on foot, ragged, hungry and cold. The mid November air was unseasonably mild, but not suited for spending daylight hours in marches, or hiding under shrubs, covered with wet autumn leaves until coveted darkness came to allow a safer passage. Confrontations with armed border guards resulted in serious injury, capture or sometimes death. The lucky ones who did not drown in the ice-cold waters of streams, or pass out from total exhaustion, did eventually appear on the west side of the border to be picked up by the Austrian border patrol and the Red Cross.

There was a stranded passenger train near Kledering, only a few kilometers from the border. Ken was informed that all the coaches were jam-packed with refugees, that food and water were badly needed, and yes, an engine to pull the train into Vienna. A staff car took Ken and his small group to the site to join the rescue effort. Fortunately, their driver spoke English.

9

"If my name is not Molnar, who am I?" she asked. Her tears were dried now and the chilly air reached to her bones. The anguish of this discovery just added to the strenuous night march to the Austrian border. Standing around now, waiting for their border guides to return, Frank held on to her even though he could have used some support himself. It was also difficult for him to give information to her that would twist her identity into a different direction. But he had to tell her. For her sake.

"According to the documents I discovered, there was a Sarah and Emanuel Klein who had a baby girl, named Erika, on May fifth in 1941" Frank reported. "This one we know for sure." They moved somewhat away from the rest of the group, out of earshot. "The rest is speculation, based on our history books. If your father was a merchant, it is possible that he owned the butcher shop or the whole building, for that matter. There were several retail places downstairs, weren't there?" he continued. "Your Molnar grandfather, as you knew him, probably worked the shop for your family. Emanuel went to war, not necessarily on his own accord; Jews at that time were digging the trenches on the frontlines, you remember? If he escaped the war and made it back, he could also have made it to America as well. But surely, you won't find anyone under the Molnar name there."

To this point it all seemed very logical to Erika. It opened up the possibility for hope and miraculous expectation that, even if incredibly distant, she may still have a family. And how about her mother? She had not come home one summer day, and drowned in the Danube, as the family was told. But during that very same time, thousands of Jews were arrested and deported, never to be seen again. History classes informed her that nazi atrocities shocked Europe at that time, not to be forgotten or forgiven. Had this been her mother's fate?

The other details of the documents seemed to explain things. Now she knew exactly where her position was in society. She did not have to hide behind her face; all she had to do was accept her past. Slowly, from her cardigan's pocket, she pulled out her gray student card, that had been issued by the Hungarian People's Republic, giving her free public transportation to her school. Free transportation that she didn't need any more. She dropped it on the ground without looking. With her heel she dug a small trench and her documented identity was unceremoniously buried, somewhere near the Austrian border, in the middle of a moonless night in early November of 1956. And at the same time, when 'Erika Molnar' disappeared from the face of the earth, more long caravans of dark Russian tanks were rumbling over Hungary's eastern border unopposed. The spontaneous uprising of a small courageous nation had rapidly been quashed.

Facing the western border, Erika Klein grabbed on to Frank Barna with newly discovered confidence. She knew, that now she was ready, but was the feeble young man she was holding on to, was he ready to begin their new lives together? The cushioned footsteps approaching from the darkness ahead brought her back to the present.

"We have good news," said one of the arriving guides. "The lights from the left are coming from a new state farm, just opened. Not that they will welcome you there, but it is a visible beacon to avoid. The border is less than a half kilometer straight ahead."

The group moved in unison. Like a huge magnet, the expectation of western freedom drew them effortlessly. No one felt tired anymore, not hungry nor even scared. Crossing that tiny line out there in the dark was the most important task in everyone's lives. It would not take long.

"There is a small detail left," said the other guide now. "We would not mind to be compensated for our successful efforts."

"We would like to get a little closer to that red-white-red flag stuck in the ground, the actual Austrian border, you know," the previous group leader spoke up.

"Maybe a few more steps, that's all," the guide said. "Don't forget, we are staying behind here, and could suffer grave consequences. We can only stand here and watch your happy crossing." He stretched out both his arms in expectation, and one by one, refugees walked up to the three of them. They began to remove their wristwatches, empty their wallets and pockets, and take off their fur coats and felt hats, some even their so needed winter coats to give. There was not one thank you said, or an exchange of words of any kind. They all knew that from now on, their silence would be their lifesaver, the donations of their worldly possessions their utmost gratitude. Spread out not more than four abreast they made determined, solemn steps toward freedom.

The first flare shot up not more than fifty meters away on the left. The sky was illuminated and revealed a row of soldiers of unknown nationality on the ground. The second flare went up not more than ten seconds later, the third and many more came in rapid succession. Startled in the open field, surrounded obviously by their enemy, chaotic running and shouting ensued. Gunfire rattled into the center, cutting down those too stunned to dive down or not brave enough to run.

The stunned fugitives faced the soldiers standing guard in a horseshoe shape, covering the western front and the sides; the rear to the east seemed to be the only way out. But who would give up all their struggles without at least trying the impossible? To escape they must run, or crawl if it proved to be safer. The guides were long gone by now, leaving their prey to the mercy of military might. The Russian circle drew smaller and smaller under the bright light of the flares above. The soldiers aimed their weapons up to the sky now, closing in to round up their petrified herd.

A strong hand grabbed Erika's arm. It was Eddy. Slowly he turned her around, making a deliberate move to the east. "I have enough natural cavities on my body, I don't care for artificial ones; do you?" They were taking quicker strides now, heading toward a row of objects that turned out to be a field of haystacks. About a half dozen more refugees followed their lead. Near the stacks, where knee deep loose hay covered the ground, Erika lost her balance. Her ankle gave out with excruciating pain. She did not want to get up. As she was lying there, face down in agony, she did not see that Frank Barna, trying to catch up with them, fell to the ground, lifeless.

"Frank... I want Frank," she moaned. Somehow she managed to turn on her side and sit up. Eddy was at the side of the haystack an arm's length away, furiously ripping out the wet, slippery material to dig a cavity. Others followed his lead, and by the time he dragged Erika in and covered the opening, there were no refugees to be seen.

It was painful, but still necessary to let Erika know of Frank's fate. Eddy clearly saw the grotesque twist of Frank's face, the involuntary rise of his arm as he fell forward and no more movement after that. The son of a high-ranking Communist official perished from the bullets of his Russian comrades. 'If you are not with us, you are against us,' became the official verdict and justification for prompt execution, even if the other casualties were not deserving of such punishment.

While the others hid under wet hay, the last lone member of their group stayed outside in the shadows for hours. He witnessed in silent disbelief how his countrymen were rounded up and loaded into military trucks indiscriminately together with the wounded and the deceased; how commands in the dreaded language of the oppressors filled the air only a few meters away. He saw the monstrous vehicles pulling away one by one, dangerously close to the heads that were desperately hiding below. When all turned quiet, he moved around to find that the commotion had moved over to the supposed state farm. Daybreak was near when tension and cold forced him to call on the others.

"They are all gone, you can come out now," he noted in a firm voice. "It will be daylight pretty soon, we better get moving." Slow movements and rustles came from the haystacks. There were only seven in the group, five men and two women. They knew that their game was over. With the overwhelming chance to be killed or get caught, it made no sense to try crossing the border again. The decision to return to their homes came with remorse. They gave it their best, and they had lost.

Erika's twisted ankle felt somewhat better; only a small limp reminded her of her ordeal. The loss of Frank hurt much more. She took the blame for all the death and destruction that had come so suddenly into their short lives and she accepted her misery as deserved punishment for being born. She knew she could never love again; losing Frank was too overwhelming. Whatever lay ahead, would have no importance at all without him.

Eddy walked quietly behind her, so as not to disturb her thoughts. He sensed that her mourning would take up all the space in her heart; he could not interfere with that. Around the bend in the country road where they walked, a row of small houses in a village appeared. The lone, single man stopped the procession.

"Listen. I am all by myself; I have no one to worry over me. It is only fair that I risk what's ahead. Stay here quietly, and if I do not return in a reasonable time, avoid this village." Without any discussion or farewell, he disappeared in the dim light. No one ever learned his name.

But reasonable time cannot be measured on a clock. Standing in the cold in desperation took its toll. Erika passed out. One of the men took a small flask from his inner pocket. The life saving palinka came to her rescue again. Eddy sat next to her on the half frozen ground, holding her limp torso in his arms.

"I must get her into a warm place," he said briefly. "Will you watch over her until I get back?" He left the shivering girl there and he too disappeared without waiting for approval.

The only light came through the smoked up little window of a blacksmith's shop. Eddy cracked the large clumsy door open and peered in. In the far corner a man with a heavy hide apron was building up a fire with bellows. He did not turn when he said, "You did not make it!"

Eddy tried to explain his embarrassing situation, their failed efforts to renounce their homeland, the desperate pain of hunger and cold. The blacksmith said that he would wake the cook of the collective farm where they had ventured, and to bring the others. Even if giving up here was equally dangerous, Eddy knew that it was their only hope for survival.

From the tiny room in the back of the farm's kitchen a middle aged woman appeared in a haggard housecoat. Without a word she began to make a fire in the wood stove, to brew coffee and warm up some old biscuits. Erika and the other girl from their group found solace in the bed the cook had just abandoned. Lying there fully clothed under the covers, only the warmth mattered.

By the time the food was ready and the group was fed, the manager of the farm arrived for his regular duty. He did not show any surprise, he did not question the legitimacy of his uninvited guests.

"All we need is a ride to the railroad station," one of the ex-refugees said. "We do not mean harm to anyone, and if we must be punished for our deeds, so be it. If there is a God above, justice will prevail."

The manager did not confirm, nor deny the request. In a low tone of voice he instructed someone, most likely his foreman, to load up the only open flatbed on one of the transport tractors and get rid of these people.

"Don't forget to stop at Section Three," he shouted after the foreman, "there is still some dry hay there to fill up the bed. And get some raincoats out for these people; it's starting to drizzle. What stupid weather we're having." He turned toward his office.

The tractor's engine coughed a few times and began to warm up. Section Three turned out to be a bunch of haystacks where two other workers waited for the flatbed. When a sufficient amount was loaded, the refugees were instructed to lie down as comfortably as they could, and to be ready for a long ride. They knew the railroad couldn't be that far.

The two helpers stood spread eagled on the top of their cargo. Rolling slowly on the farm's dirt road a one sided conversation ensued from the two men. They informed those buried in the hay below when they left the farmyard proper, when they passed the cornfields that still needed harvesting, and they warned of the humps of small bridges over dried out streams. Then came the watchtowers. The western border of Hungary, protected from imperialist invasion, was downscaled from fields of landmines to high wooden structures about half a kilometer apart where sentries surveyed the countryside.

The manager also knew how to time this little maneuver. Ahead of his escapees, but not too far ahead of them, was the food wagon carrying the guard's anticipated breakfast. As the soldiers vacated their posts to consume their food at the bottom of the tower's stairs, the farm workers greeted them in their particular language, signaling to their cargo the multi-nationality of the defenders of communism.

The sun was up now, quickly burning up all the mist in the air, shining through the boards of the loosely built towers to indicate who was manning his post and who wasn't. At the appropriate spot the tractor stopped. The wagon's western side was lowered, and instructions came in muffled voices.

"Slide down and walk. Not too fast, but steady. You have fifty meters to cover. God be with you."

The coveted flag of Austria swayed in the distance. Remnants of the barbed wire fence that was built along the border could still be seen; parts of the disturbed ground of the old minefields were also visible. The refugees lowered their torsos and bent their knees as they shuffled towards freedom. Only their eyes twinkled with gratitude to their kind helpers; there was nothing left to give. When the rattle of a machinegun burst over the flatland, the tempo of their exit turned into a desperate dash for their lives. They did not see that the farm workers were cut down next to their flatbed; they only saw the flapping of the red-white-red of the Austrian flag coming closer and closer.

Would the Russian Army break international laws and fire into the territory of a neutral country? Would they be satisfied enough with murdering their own subjects? No one questioned all this, only desperately hoped for the better. In the thickness of the nearby shrubs they searched for refuge. It seemed all six of them made it.

Not far behind in the distance, with the morbid truth of reality, the tractor's engine purred in idle submission. Further to the east, a whole nation surrendered to their fate of defeat. Many lives were lost, thousands of families broken up, but their immense sacrifice did not really change anything. Change was only for those who made it across the temporarily dysfunctional Iron Curtain.

The small white transport bus with a large red cross on its sides slowly labored down the dirt road ahead. At a safe distance the vehicle stopped, and the driver stepped out. Waving with both arms, he signaled welcome to Austria.

10

"Willcommen!" said the Austrian bus driver in a soft voice as the refugees walked up the steps in single file. Standing next to his seat, he turned toward the middle of the bus. In a strong foreign accent but understandable Hungarian, he continued. "We do this every morning, you see. Drive around and pick up you *fluhtlings*. Sometimes more, sometimes less. I am glad you have made it. We are your friends and good neighbors, please accept all we are able to give you."

When the new got on the bus, most of the seats had already been taken. The passengers were a wide mixture of old and young, some better dressed than others, some happy, others depressed, but all were somewhat confused. They all knew, deep in their hearts, that leaving their homeland was necessary to avoid retribution from their communist government. Leaving family and friends behind, breaking up their careers, their education, and their total life structure began to settle in their minds. Yes, they seemed to be safe now, but they had heard only bad things about the west. That most westerners had harsh lives without the support and protection of a strong governmental system; they were known to still live in slavery. Slaving for their imperialist-capitalist overlords exploiting every muscle in their bodies, every ounce of their brains.

So, why did they risk their lives, sacrifice their sheltered existence for a darkly drawn, foreign future? Was all the filtered information on life outside the socialist cocoon believable? They had just failed their attempt to shake off the chains of controlled collectivism; would this final leap to assumed freedom also be a failure?

The driver scoured the eastern countryside to make sure no one was left out of his morning run. "Now, lets go for lunch. There is a nice restaurant up in the village," he said with a twinkle in his eyes.

He was kidding, of course, but he was right. They drove to an old tavern that was probably ancient by the last century. Its white stucco walls had attracted travelers for a very long time. A large oak gate, with an ellipse shape top awaited, open for the new arrivals. A passageway led to a large square courtyard. A hand cranked well and long concrete trough accented its simple interior. Numerous doors opened to different rooms on all sides. Surrounding the courtyard was a narrow, overhead canopy, which protected the long table where several caldrons of hearty soup steamed in the noon sun. Baskets of sliced, heavy Austrian bread rounded out the menu. By the time the starving crowd received their small bowls of warm soups, another busload arrived to queue up in their desperate need for nourishment.

There was no place to sit, no need to order, no menu to chose from, and no bill to pay. Even swill would have tasted great now, as long as it was warm. They stood around the walls of the courtyard, not talking, just devouring their gift. Another Hungarian speaking person came to the center to give instructions about their immediate future. The tavern, for all practical purposes was closed to the public, and for the past few days, it had become the collection center for refugees.

"You are *Fluchtlings* now, refugees in our safe home," the man said. It was truly amazing how the Austrians gathered so many volunteers in such a very short time. Some spoke in a broken language, yet were able to communicate with so many people pouring into their country; although the border towns and villages of Austria, separated from Hungary some forty years ago, still had older people who spoke their neighbor's tongues. The large central space, a grand ballroom, so to speak, with oiled floor and a cast-iron stove in the middle was a gathering place for local youths on Saturday nights. Now it was turned into a huge, community bedroom. Dry straw was spread lavishly around the floor, coarse horse blankets, probably by courtesy of the Austrian Cavalry, became dozens of makeshift beds. An extra blanket was given to each refugee as they entered the room and they were asked to find space and comfort as best as they could. Several outhouses could be reached through a door leaving the building; ice-cold water in the trough served as a huge bathroom sink. The refugees took their primitive public baths by dipping into the trough with their palms, splashing their faces, turning away to let the water drip on the ground so as not to soil the rest.

Eddy never left Erika's side. He held her elbow on the short walk to the bus, sat next to her and was behind her in the chow line. They ate silently, gulping down the warm, heavy soup spiced with an unfamiliar taste of Maggi, a dark brown liquid flavoring popular in this country.   The earthenware bowls were collected and one by one, the refugees entered the bedroom. Eddy stretched his neck to locate an empty spot. Behind the brick chimney of the stove there was a small area of bare floor. He knelt and grabbed handfuls of straw from the foot side of their neighbors' beds, not much, just enough to cushion the hard pine, and some more to form pillows. He covered it all with the blanket he had just received. Erika's allotment was folded for a headrest and Eddy's jacket marked their spot as taken. Now they were able to tour the facility.

Service at the bar was naturally closed now. The tables were pulled together in rows and fellow countrymen were already comforting themselves at friendly card games. With their stomachs full and having a warm place to sleep, the memories of war and their struggles temporarily faded from their minds. There were no plans for the future yet, the past was momentarily forgotten, and so they began to enjoy the present. Under the warmth of the afternoon sun, Eddy held Erika's hand as they strolled out of the tavern. She did not pull away.

The center of the town seemed to be only a short walk away. They admired the neat, spacious homes Austrians lived in, even in this small village; the clean courtyards, the nice front gardens adorned with late blooming flowers. It was like a fairytale. They enjoyed the fresh air and the bright colors pleased their eyes. If this was freedom, it might be good.

"It must be a Roman Catholic church," Eddy said as he opened the heavy door. "Look at all the colorful statues of saints. I believe the whole country here is Catholic." She did not remember ever being in a church. Her confirmation was staged in a photo studio, not wanting to antagonize the authorities. It was a private matter her grandfather schemed up, perhaps to save her soul for the afterlife. The flickering candles against the cool walls of this stone church gave a mysterious feeling. She knelt in the front of the altar. She felt the need to say thanks in a prayer, if she only knew how. And suddenly it came to her.

"Our Father which art in Heaven, Give us our daily bread..." she began. The words came in English. She remembered this much although she knew it wasn't all of it or even correct. She had learned it when she was much younger. She knew an old woman in their building back home, a retired nun, who taught English before the war. Of the few hundred English words she had learned from her, the very first, she now remembered, was the Lord's Prayer. She cried quietly for a few minutes, then she realized knowing some English would be part of her salvation on this earth, if only God would provide the rest. While kneeling there in the sanctuary of a supreme being, she worked to recall other English words she had learned, nothing to do with prayers. Words like church, God, candles and flowers, then boy, girl, happiness and struggle. The words came, in random order, slowly at first, and then surprisingly fast. Even though knowing German would have been more important now, she felt that in the very near future English would be more useful. What if her father would not understand Hungarian any more? What if there was no father at all in America?

Walking around the small town square, the commercial center of the village, they found it odd that all the stores were closed so early in the afternoon, only to realize that their first day of freedom fell on a Sunday.

Shouts from the tavern brought them back to reality. A large bus was parked out front and the crowd pushed hard to get into it. No one cared where it might be going, or if there was order in the proceedings; all they wanted was to get on with their lives. Erika could not yet run on her injured ankle. Although Eddy eagerly tried to help, by the time they got to their lodging, the bus had pulled away.

"So what?" Eddy assured her, "They must have others coming. Besides, look at all the room we will have, even more food later." He headed back to the main room. It seemed the buses must have left empty since there were just as many people there as before. Fortunately, their spot was still open. He asked Erika to sit with him. There was so much to tell.

"I was going to be an actor," he began his biography. "Maybe even an opera singer. But my father was a high-ranking administrator in city government before the war. Isn't it interesting that we all have two lives. One before the war and one after. Anyway, he is now pumping gas for this regime at the outskirts of our capital on the highway to Vienna. He was all right, we somehow survived it, but his past was detrimental to my education. There were plenty of intellectuals in our country already, so I was destined to become an Agronomist. Imagine, me plowing dirt or even walking in dirt? Now I'm here," he went on. "I think I will go to Italy, but they have too many singers there already. No, I must go to Hollywood. I shall do that."

Erika did not know what to say or do. Should she tell him something or everything about her life? Should she be exposed needlessly to everyone who talked to her? Lies are not easy to tell, she thought. You must remember every lie you told, so as not to be caught the next time around. And she knew she was lying when she said she was eighteen. Was she lying when she said she was Jewish or did that lie come from someone else? Then again, is it safe to be Jewish in a German speaking country? Is it right to say you are eighteen when one doesn't know how to be that old?

She did not want to talk anymore. If only she could sleep a little.

Eddy understood. He stood up and went to the bar to play cards, or just contemplate the future in America, alone, quietly, hopefully. When he returned to the room several hours later, most of the refugees had retired, stretched out on top of their makeshift beds, fully clothed, not because they were bashful, but to be prepared when the next bus arrived. They tossed and turned in this new and strange environment; some snored and many talked in their sleep. Eddy carefully snuggled up to Erika quietly, trying not to wake her; after all, he had not been invited to share her bed, even if it was his handiwork that had prepared it. He had never slept with a girl before. Lying there on his side, watching her breasts moving up and down with each breath, the smell of her body from this close felt exciting. He knew that there must be more to it, but not now, not here. He closed his eyes hard, waiting for sleep to come.

Daylight came soon and so did the buses from the border again. A fresh load of brave but exhausted souls rushed to the food line. In the meantime, members of the Red Cross worked cautiously in the large bedroom. Section by section they led small sleepy groups to the barroom to be fed milk and fresh bread. Through the kitchen's back door, empty buses began to load them up. A new day, another step toward the west resumed. Nobody knew where, only that it was now.

Once a bus emptied of new arrivals, was driven around the building and stopped at the back door Red Cross workers assembled a new crowd from the bedroom and escorted them to the bus. There were no 'good-byes' or 'thank yous' exchanged as they parted. The helpers were too busy; the helped didn't know what to say. By the time Erika took the seat that Eddy was saving for her, several more vehicles were lined up behind them. The caravan proceeded out to the main road. When the first white bus turned onto Highway 10 excited words were passed among the passengers. "We are going to Vienna," said the ones who were better versed in Austrian geography. Passing through the town of Bruck verified their assumption. They knew by now that there was a large camp in the outskirts of Vienna where all Hungarian refugees were gathered for processing. From there, they could go anywhere they wished, they were told, and the whole world was the limit.

Eddy stuck to Erika like she was a magnet. He felt fortunate that other guy was gone, even if it had to be so tragically definite. Life must go on, he thought, you never know when your turn comes, so make the best of it. He began to chatter, for he was a blabbermouth, always had been. Maybe that's what made him so advanced in school; he felt he had to explain everything to everybody. He was also fun to be with. He always knew the proper joke that went with the subject of the conversation, or a story about something, real or otherwise.

"Have you ever been to the Balaton?" he asked Erika.

"Of course, who hasn't? My parents had a cottage in Foldvar." She did remember that, when she was a toddler, soaking her little feet in the crystal clear waters on the south side of the largest lake in Europe. But if that was true and not a story, her family had to be well off. She had learned in history class how the affluent upper class of Hungary kept a fashionable apartment in the capital, and a cozy villa somewhere for the family to spend the summers on a lake. A butcher could never do that. Her family must have been rich, even if it came with being Jewish.

"How interesting. I spent many summers there," Eddy said, interrupting her thoughts. "Only in a tent, of course, but a large one at that. My older brother took us kids for weeks at a time to clean off city dust. Which reminds me of a story, a true, honest-to-goodness episode," he went on, no holds barred. It happened during the first summer after the war ended. Wooden walkways extended from the shore of the lake far into the water, over the belt of huge rocks that protected the seawall. Steps at the end of the deck let you enter the water safely, even if that part was still shallow.

"We used to run like crazy and jump off the deck, not wasting time with steps," Eddy recalled. "About ten steps away in the water, protruding from the sand was this skinny stump. You could miss it if you were careful, but still it was quite a hazard." He went on with the story about a bunch of kids deciding to get the stump out. The old trick of physics applied, all you had to do was to move your palms forcefully over the object, and let the water wash out the surrounding sand. The south side of the lake was nothing but sand.

"You should have seen the surprise we had. It wasn't a stump at all. It was a stupid row-boat." Their task became a bit too much. Recruiting some local boys, preferably older ones, was the answer. And they worked, dug feverously, on all sides until a good chunk of the vessel was out of the sand. It was then that one of the big boys suggested communal lifting of one side.

"And it happened," Eddy continued. "Under force, a big chunk of the boat's edge broke off. The kids stood up and examined their catch. Beneath the corroded wooden rim of the boat chunks of yellow soap bars were visible."

"Oh my Lord! It's dynamite!" someone shouted. Quick did not describe the scattering that took place. Within seconds, there was nobody in the water. The nearest telephone was a few hundred meters away, at the shack where railroad people activated the street crossing gates. The man on duty called the Stationmaster; he in turn called the police. They did not need an explanation. This was not the first such case.

During the war, Lake Balaton was a natural barrier

between the Soviets on the south and Germans on the north side of the lake. The locals are still laughing about how the stupid Russian tanks entered the shallow waters of the south beach and got stuck a half a kilometer into the lake. But it was too late by then, and it was only after numerous losses of their fine equipment that they realized the need for water vessels. In turn, the Germans created a conniving means of defense, mounting a good amount of dynamite on simple wooden rowboats and letting them loose at night. When the Russian pontoons tried to sneak to the north shore, a good many of them hit the explosives.

The police did not take the responsibility of disarming the rowboat the boys had found. Their call went straight to the Army in Siofok, and to the Lake Patrol in Tihany. Within an hour armed boats circled the water side, and infantry closed down the beach. No one actually could guess the size of the dynamite, or gauge its ability to destroy the whole town.

"But you made it," Erika said almost deliberately intercepting the flow of words. He took the hint and glanced out the window. The refugee buses had left the main road. Along small parcels of farmland they labored slowly now on narrow passages. Conversations on the bus diminished into silence; all eyes were on the road ahead. Are they negotiating a roadblock? Are the Austrians taking them back to Hungary? Pessimism set in on the petrified passengers. Some began swearing at the Austrian Government, and at the Americans for allowing such treachery. Crossing several railroad tracks, staring at the flat emptiness in front of them, their worst fear felt closer. Now the lead bus made a sharp turn and rolled down the dirt road along the tracks. Behind a row of bald acacia trees, the rear end of a passenger train appeared. Pulling alongside, the bus stopped and the doors opened. Eight cars of the train were waiting for them.

It was obvious now that the most effective way of transporting all these people had to be on rails, even if this particular train was lacking an engine. Without commands or instructions, the subdued passengers left the buses and approached the train. It seemed all the windows were open and full of spectators. The buses left as quietly as they had come, and the newcomers headed to the steps of the train. The people on the train explained that they had been there for two days now, that nothing was moving, and more and more buses were arriving. The stench of human excrement nauseated people walking by. While the coaches had a toilet at each end, in transit and normal conditions, there was water to flush. But here, everything fell to the ground, creating ever-growing ugly humps under the cars. There were no holding tanks on the trains and no water.

Eventually, they all realized their predicament and remembered the causes that had brought them all here. They began to share spaces as much as they could, even scraps of food the new group salvaged. A constant flow and movement finally made an unpleasant situation bearable. It was then that someone noticed the waving arms far on the other side of the tracks. While the train station was visible from here, they were still isolated from civilization. Crossing the four sets of tracks, some of the refugees ventured closer. On the other side of the concrete fence that bordered railroad property, there was a small house, its owner trying to get their attention. A garden hose protruding through the fence provided a constant trickle of drinking water. A long row of refugees developed carrying any container imaginable to collect the life saving liquid. All the thanks in Hungarian, and welcomes in German, were exchanged in spite of the language barrier.

The afternoon sun was getting lower, somewhere above the coveted city of Vienna. The air got chillier too; getting comfortable for another night of anxious waiting was on everyone's mind. With horror, the passengers near the road saw another caravan of vehicles approaching. Off the first bus several uniformed figures emerged. It was the International Red Cross. Behind them, boxes and boxes of something were unloaded with deliberate haste. Nobody knew, until the first container was opened, that a huge supply of dried, chubby, Austrian sausages had arrived.

Elation can be expressed with loud screams and shouts. They are the international language of joy that is felt after exhausting stress and cannot be found not in dictionaries. Yet there was no commotion. Movements stalled and bodies squeezed closer to make room for the angels in bluish gray uniform to do their heavenly mission. Food, that eluded them for so long, had finally arrived. It did not matter that it was only a small piece of sausage and nothing else. It was delicious even if its spices were foreign to the Hungarian palate. No one dared to ask for a second piece to stash away for future emergencies because they felt that from now on, life would always be better. When the next truck arrived with fresh rolls an hour later, they devoured them just the same, even though all the sausages were gone by then.

The shock jolted the train, almost knocking over those who were standing. The second impact sent them in the other direction. Instant applause echoed through the train; they all knew that their locomotive had arrived. The beginning of movement transformed the sorrowful crowd into a joyful gang like that of sports fans who were going home from a winning game. Some even turned to the countryside and began to notice how orderly Austrian farms were and how clean the stockyards and stables were as they passed. The politically free west suddenly became physically pretty as well. In less than an hour their train pulled into the *Sudbanhof* of Vienna.

The numerous concrete elevated platforms between the tracks, and there were quite a few of them, were protected from the elements by metal roofs and provided a view of a long, well lit tunnel which was suddenly busy. On small tables in equal intervals along the total length of the train, lay containers of cookies and hot chocolate, drinking water and more small rolls, round and crusty in brilliant display. This well presented meal was received as royal feast. It was time to move about and leave the confinement of the train; it felt good to stroll and enjoy refreshments. Vienna put out all this food in short notice. From the home city of the imperial Hapsburgs from which they had ruled over half the world for seven centuries, the people of Austria sent a message of welcome to a large group of discontented children of social oppression. Two whistles from the engine shook their minds back to reality as they scurried back to take their places on the train.

After an hour of speeding through empty farmland under the dark, starless November night, the sad truth became evident. If there was a large refugee camp in Vienna, this train was not going there. A tall, young man in the uniform of the American Red Cross entered the coach almost unnoticed. His friendly face looked tired; his eyes searched the semidarkness of the interior. He made a few unsure steps, balancing himself on the tops of benches. Ken Williams was taking inventory of his charges. He was far from his comfortable Connecticut home, and thoroughly at a loss for words.

"English!" he almost shouted, "Does anyone speak English?" Why he trained his gaze into the far corner, he never knew, but there was this young girl, her large hazel eyes staring through the dark window of the train, unaware of the strange, big world reflecting back to her. Her short, brown hair, unkempt in tangles, half covered the soft white skin of her pretty face. She turned slowly in a daze toward the American.

"I speak," she said almost to herself. For Erika Klein knew that the few English words she remembered could not be much help. Perhaps only in a prayer. But Ken was moving close with obvious relief.

"I am Ken, from America, to help you. Would you tell your countrymen that we are going to the far end of Austria, and we should be in Tirol by the morning."

While she tried her best, interpreting was almost unnecessary. The word Tirol and the word morning registered perfectly in the refugee's minds; all they needed now was a good night's sleep. Outside, unbeknownst to most of the passengers, the mountains of Salzburg loomed in quiet majesty in the distance. And probably for all of them, this was the closest they had ever been to West Germany, the much talked about symbol of the free western world. Tirol was just as good now, even if no one guessed why they were going there.

11

Under the darkness of the night, the overloaded train labored across most of Austria unnoticed. At Linz, they mercifully got a stronger, electric powered locomotive, more accustomed to climbing higher altitudes and negotiating long tunnels. At Salzburg, they stopped again, to attach a boxcar to the train loaded with more provisions for the refugees. By morning, when they passed through Innsbruck, the capital of Tirol, the sun had come up and the clouds had disappeared. The Alps loomed over both sides of the valley like surrogate aunts protecting children not their own. Mother Nature placed tall peaks, some over 2500 meters, at regular intervals to help mankind measure distances. Sitting high, they proudly showed their white caps that they wore year around.

From here the tracks seemed to be going upward; it was unlikely that the mountains were getting smaller. But the valley was definitely getting narrower, guiding the Inn River towards the sea, rushing in the opposite direction. Here and there whitecaps waved to the refugees in the brilliant morning light.

With nothing else to do, some of the passengers tried to guess their location and read the strange names on railroad station signs as they zoomed through. Some knew with certainty, that Hungary was at least 500 kilometers to the east by now; and when they stopped again, it was the little town of Imst, another name nobody had heard of before. Ski runs sloped down the sides of the mountains, empty of snow, for the unusual winter of 1956 should have already been here, and yet, at the bottom of the valleys, fields of grain showed off their pretty green blankets. The train stopped and did not move again.

Red Cross workers began to usher people out of the compartments. Gathering on the platform, they had the feeling that they had arrived to their destination. A short, chubby man in his late fifties gathered up his American Red Cross colleagues. His long winter coat seemed unnecessary; the weather was playing a fair game.

"I'm Wynn," he introduced himself to Ken and the rest of the staff when they met. "I am the Commandant of this camp. How many have you brought?"

"Two, maybe three hundred, we won't know until we take a headcount. Can we handle it?"

"Can anyone speak with these people?" the Commandant wanted to know ignoring the question.

"Yes, one of the refugees is a Shakespearian actor," Ken replied. "I have problems understanding him sometimes, but he is the best we have. There is a young girl also, but she is not the greatest either. You know, those bastard communists forbade the learning of English in Hungary on the grounds that it is the language of dirty imperialists."

"We will fight that problem for a while, I am sure," the chief went on, "but I do have a Hungarian here to assist me. He is an ex-military guy who got stuck in this country after the war. He is also the one who will set up security for us. This many people need to be controlled by their own folks, I believe. He has a British accent and not much tact, but maybe in time his vocabulary or his attitude will improve.

The camp is about two miles from here, and uphill at that. Are they strong enough to make the climb on foot? I am quite short of transportation, you know. But before we start, let me say a few welcoming words to them."

The refugees were assembled to form a thick ring around the American. He raised his arm and waited patiently for silence. "How Do You Do?" he began his speech. He informed the crowd that the French Barracks in Warben, a nearby village not on the rail line, was refurbished to be their home away from home. French troops were stationed here during World War II and the compound had been abandoned until now. He asked for their patience and their help to make it livable. Rations would be provided, he promised, and clothing, courtesy of the kind people of Western Europe, would be available; and of course, cooked meals and hot tea would be served as soon as they got there. The actor grasped for the right words in modern English. Out of the short welcoming ceremony there were only two things that stuck in everybody's mind, "warm food," and that their camp Commandant's name was "HowDoYouDo."

The little village of Warben, developed around the old military camp, was mostly made up of small dairy farms, a general store, a five room *Gausthaus* with a small restaurant, and of course, a tiny Chapel. The builders of the narrow streets were stingy with their efforts, making the few intersections barely navigable. The line of tired refugees snaking from the railroad station moved slowly toward the hillside. From the few houses along the way, curious people were assessing their new neighbors.

The compound resembled an eighteenth-century fort, its stone, two story buildings enclosed by a large, rectangle courtyard. A wooden gate, big enough for vehicle traffic, could be closed up for the night. Construction timber had aged since it was hastily built and the mortar had crumbled from the harsh mountain weather, but the insides, which could have used a fresh coat of whitewash if time and the extra expense had allowed it, was livable. The first structure to the right held the office, kitchen and a warehouse. The other buildings were simple sleeping quarters, small rooms with a wood stove in each, and a bath large enough to serve all the soldiers on each floor. The furthest building in the yard was an open sided large barn where firewood and fresh straw were stored.

A few concrete steps and a small balcony formed the entrance to the office building. A middle-aged man in the uniform of the prewar Hungarian Army leaned against the railing, puffing on his third cigarette. He looked over the gathering crowd, a strange expression on his face, like he was not sure if he was counting sheep or searching for someone special. The Camp Commandant walked up to him and turned toward the people as a signal. The Army man raised both his arms and shouted.

"Attention everybody! Attention!" Faces turned and mouths closed at the loud voice, but at least it was Hungarian. "Call me Lieutenant Ronay. I am your Sub-Commandant, basically in charge here. I do not need any interpreter to tell you what to do, which makes things a bit easier. I expect strict obedience and respect for the rules of this camp. To form a Security Force, I need a few volunteers. Please come forward now. Zoltan here, my Assistant," and pointed to a smaller man at the bottom of the stairs, "will take care of you." He stopped abruptly and moved to meet his Security Force.

Now it was Zoltan's turn to step up to his boss' place to bark his orders.

"People," he began, " I want you to make the

following groups. Families here, single men there, and women over there," pointing in different directions in the courtyard. As the crowd started to move, he turned to a confused woman. "Where do you belong?"

"I am a widow."

"Well? If you are alone, get with the girls. Say, lady, where is your husband?" he asked another.

"I don't have one."

"Oh? And where is the big belly from?"

"Why don't you stick your nose in it?" hollered a girl angrily behind the pregnant one. "Come on with us Susie," and she put her arms around the now weeping woman.

There was another girl in the yard, standing alone, a bit away from the crowd, a brunette teenager with the shape of a grown woman but the innocent face of a child. She had no luggage, not even a pocketbook. The girl who spoke before came up to her.

"Hey, call me Blackie. Are you with somebody?" she asked with a smile.

She sadly shook her head.

"Now, listen to me, kid," she said motherly. "The storm is over, the house is gone, the stove, grandma and the boy next door, are all gone. Only you are here. Now pull yourself together and let's settle down somewhere." Each group slowly made its way toward their designated quarters. Blackie escorted her protégées to their new home and closed the door.

"How many mattresses do we have?" she asked searching around the room. Rough, hemp sacks filled with straw and covered with blankets lay around the walls. Next to the door, away from the makeshift sleeping provisions, an unlit cast-iron stove was the only other furnishing.

"There are ten," one of the quicker girls reported the inventory, "for eleven of us."

"Hey, Sad Eyes, you come with me," Blackie commanded, "I think I know where they all come from." She turned back from the door, "This room is full. Don't let anybody in, you understand?"

The hallway was crowded with busy people looking for familiar faces and for assigned rooms. Blackie took over the leadership without opposition. Some of the girls even thought that the Camp Commandant appointed her for the job.

"You know, I don't even know your name," Blackie said as they took to the stairs.

"Molnar Erika." It just came out, without thinking, a familiar part of her true life, and it was too late now to become Klein again, a strange name she could not get used to, or even like. It was the first time she had spoken since she got separated from Eddy. She wasn't sure if she wanted to look for him, he was with all the other men now, but if she really needed to, she knew she could find him.

Blackie had spied the barn in the back earlier where the straw mattresses were made, that is if you were a strong, young man. Being a fragile but attractive woman, you had to do it differently. That is what Blackie didn't know how to do just yet. But the answer came along by itself as they stepped out of the building. On the now snowless grounds, there was a nicely shaped mattress walking on two legs in a wrinkled pair of trousers toward the door. Blackie put her arms out to stop it.

"Care to tell us what time it is?" she chanced a bluff.

"Sorry, I have no watch," came the muffled answer from down under.

"Can you prove it?" Blackie went on.

"Look, who ever you are in that skirt, which is the only thing I can see now, I gave my very good wrist-watch to the man who guided me through the border. Ever since then I don't know, or even care what the time is. Now, would you be so kind as to let me pass."

"Take it easy, young man, that's good enough proof for me. Now, why don't you run down to the main building and pick up your own Swiss timepiece. I heard there are not too many left to give out."

The mattress fell to ground, and the skinny young boy dashed through the yard never looking back.

"That's cheating," Erika said nervously.

"So what, he didn't even care to look at us. Besides, he is strong enough to make another one. Now, let's take this gift home."

Even if they saved on the work of making their own mattress, it was still a heavy chore to drag it up the stairs, but it fit nicely back in the corner of the room. Covered with a blanket it became a comfortable home. Erika could hardly wait to crash down and pass out. She did not care if there was food or if it was possible to clean up. When her roommates returned, she was sound asleep, probably searching for food in her dreams.

"Good Evening," Blackie greeted her when she began to stir. "We thought you were dead already. Are you all right?"

"I don't know, but I wouldn't tell you anyway. What time is it?"

"I see you are feeling perky. The sun is down already." She filled Erika in on the events of the past few hours, and said that some provisions had been distributed at the office. She gave her what the girls picked up for her; a small bowl for her meals, a cup and some utensils, all lightweight plastic; a towel, a bar of soap, and tube of paste with her toothbrush. Erika also learned that a large kitchen provided their food, to be picked up at mealtime because where the soldiers used to eat was now the warehouse. Here, clothing donated and collected from all over the Western World, was to be sorted out and distributed to the refugees.

She was still in the clothes that she had worn running away from home; there was nothing to change into. Now she picked up her cleaning stuff and headed to the bathroom. A few minutes later she returned, shaking, as she fell through their door. "Where is our bathroom?" she asked breathlessly.

"You were there this morning."

"Where I was is full of naked men now."

The room burst out laughing. "You have to go downstairs, honey," one of the girls said. "Have you seen anything interesting?"

"So what if she did," said another, "you got a lease on them?"

"Does it bother you what someone enjoys?" somebody asked as the conversation got into a semi-argument, lightened by occasional laughter and colored with innocent blushes. Erika slipped out quietly to find the right place this time.

Although she heard distinct feminine sounds, the cheerful laughter, the rolling mass of soprano indicating that she was at the right place; Erika pushed open the bathroom door slowly, just to make sure. The long room had several gray metal toilet stalls against the walls on two sides. In the middle, a pair of galvanized troughs paralleled almost the whole length of the chamber. Several faucets serving both sides of the crude washbasin emitted plenty of cold water. Apparently, wartime soldiers had not required showers.

Women in a mixed state of attire were furiously attacking the dirt and grime that had accumulated over the several days since they had left their homes. The weird circumstance of exposing yourself in public seemed not to bother most, but Erika felt funny. Reluctantly, she removed some of her clothing, the top first, and tried to wash thoroughly. The fragrance of Ivory soap, something she had never experienced in her own country, gave a refreshing sensation. The feeling of being clean was more important to her now than the pang of hunger, for she hadn't eaten in quite some time.

She knew that soiled or not, she had nothing to change into. So, the blouse covered her again. While she thought that she needed one, she did not own a bra. Her corduroy pants had kept her warm so far and seemed all right, but she had to rinse out her panties. The few minutes it took she shivered, not sure if it was from the chilly air or from embarrassment. She managed to wring out most of the water and the wet garment went back on in a hurry. Yet, nobody paid any attention to her or anyone else. Concentration was focused on to the flow of fresh water. She did not talk to anyone in the room, and soon scurried back upstairs.

The girls stopped their silly chatter as Erika walked in. They congregated near Blackie who just raised her voice. "Girls. This is Erika, the eleventh member of our little community, and if you could be quiet for a minute, she will tell us everything about herself. Won't you Erika?"

"There is not much to tell," she began while spreading her towel on the top of her bed to dry. "My family name is Molnar," she had to concentrate on this version; " I'm eighteen," she blushed slightly from this lie; "and I have no family. I've never been married, and now I live here."

"Poor girl, she's an orphan," one of the girls remarked sadly.

"Poor? She sure is, if she's never been married," a

heavyset young woman added. "I was married once, and I'm telling you, there is nothing like it, except another one. And boy, have you seen all those single guys in the yard? They all will want to get married some day, and there are a lot to choose from," she went on nonstop. "I'm telling you, I will get after them as soon as we get some decent clothing. Then I'll show you how to catch a man in one easy lesson. I might even tell you about some other things; I've been married once you know, and there is nothing like it,"

"Just another one," somebody finally interrupted. "You might even put up a floorshow for us as soon as you get a sucker on your fat belly."

"Oh, shut up," fatso fought back, "a man can break his tool in that bonny skeleton of yours, if he would have the taste for it."

"At least he wouldn't choke to death on your huge boobs."

"But I can suffocate your dirty mouth with one, couldn't I?"

"Come on, girls," Blackie interrupted, "we don't have to disrupt this party with derogatory comments on each other's shape. The fat will get skinny and the bony bonier if we don't get some grub into the aforementioned bellies." She looked around the room until her message got through, and then appointed four girls to go and pick up their food.

The group worked hard to get their room pleasant and somewhat useable. They found enough wood in the barn to start a fire in their little stove. Somebody located a small iron bar to serve as a hammer, pulled some nails from the barn's walls with a rusty can opener, and with some scrap lumber they made shelves. Meals, always a single course, were dished out at regular times of the day, and they were eaten in their assigned rooms. The rare find of a large coffee can served as a kettle to warm water for dishwashing. Susie, with her apparent pregnancy, became an important member of the group. She was issued a somewhat banged up washbowl, and with some ingenuity they scrounged up extra blankets to create a cubicle to wash up in privacy with the luxury of warm water.

Erika was delegated to be the scout for the group; her slender, innocent youth allowed her to wander around the camp unsuspected to search out anything remotely useful in their new home. This was how she strayed into the warehouse area. There was only one door to be opened and she found herself in a very large room resembling a rummage-sale setup. She noticed a small group of men busy sorting out mountains of clothing piled up on tables. One of the men looked up curiously as she appeared in the doorway. The others stopped whatever they were doing and moved towards the door with miscellaneous articles in their hands.

"Is anything wrong?" Erika asked with an uneasy voice.

"No, no," the first man said, "It's just that we did not expect to have girls come to help us. Management is very kind to send us such a pretty young lady. We sure appreciate not only your assistance, but mainly your presence will make our job more cheerful."

At this point another man came out from the back of the room. In his late thirties, he had a well-shaped figure and friendly blue eyes. He sounded pompously intellectual.

"What he means, Miss, is that pretty girls are more likely to know a lot more about the uses and sizes of the garments of the opposite sex; we'd be very pleased to use your expertise. By the way, my name is Peter. Varga Peter. My crew here is trying diligently to get these things in order as soon as possible. You may know how badly these extra clothes are needed in the camp."

After a brief introduction, the small crew went back to work. A long table was set up near the entrance, large signs identified the type of clothing to be found there, separated for men, women and children. Sizes didn't really matter much; their selection wasn't that sophisticated. As the tables on the far side began to clear, an unending line of boxes had to be opened and unpacked. The first wave of donations, mostly from West Germany and of course Austria, began to pour in soon after the first shot was fired in the Revolution. Kindhearted people from everywhere shared their spare belongings with the unfortunates, everything from basic undergarments to fur coats and even shoelaces.

"This job will last for days if we don't get more help," Erika commented, never mentioning the fact that she wasn't sent there in the first place.

"Can't get too many people in here," Peter said, "without being in each other's way. But they could have sent a few more girls, for sure."

"I can get some," she offered, and soon Blackie and another woman joined in. Their chore soon became fun, jokes and laughter filled the room as the piles on the tables got higher and higher. They were getting close to opening up for the onslaught of needy refugees. Peter worked close by Erika all along, watching the young girl's enthusiasm and energy. Near the end of their row he looked around for a way to get out of earshot of the others.

"I admire your disciplined character," he began. "I think, with your young age and your pleasing appearance, you need it very much. Especially with the unusual situation that we are in, a young girl can easily be disoriented. When everybody is on his own, the strong could take advantage of the weak. And at that point, my child, the only protection you can have is self-discipline, which I am very glad that you have.

"Unless," and he looked around to see if anybody was listening, "unless, you have a mature friend with honorable intentions to protect you from the evils of life and from the weaknesses of human character." He stopped, waiting for a reaction to his observations. She didn't know what to say, or where all this was leading to. Peter finally made his move.

"May I be that kind of a friend to you, Erika? I am thirty-nine years old, and happily married. As a matter of fact, I have my wife with me, but she went to town with some of her lady friends. Perhaps she will be here soon and you can meet her."

"It is very nice of you Mister Varga." She tried to stop the avalanche of affection. "It seems that all the people I have met so far are on my side, kind and friendly. I can't believe that anybody would want to hurt me in any way. Thanks for your kind offer, it is an honor and I will try hard to earn it."

"Thank you, Erika. I will be your guardian angel and will make sure no one will ever hurt you. By the way, where are your quarters?"

"We are in room 21 in the C building,"

"How sad. Married couples and families are in Building B, but we are not that far from each other. Oh, before I forget, if you find anything, anything at all that fits you, don't hesitate to take it. After all, you are working hard for it."

One of the boys needed Peter's attention and they parted. She began to look closely at the items she had been working on for hours. It was interesting to find that some of the garments were her size; the pretty colors and fine materials were ones she could never afford. Even if some of the clothing was used, they all came here clean and in good condition. She had found almost everything that she could need, a couple of warmer blouses, some skirts if the weather would warm up, and a heavy winter coat which she had never owned. Underwear in sealed plastic packages was donated from a department store in Berlin. She picked up a pair of leather boots too; snow could be here any day now. She even found a small suitcase, light brown made of compressed paper, but it came as a perfect storage for her new properties.

She was ready now to face her future world, no matter how gloomy Peter described it. Help was coming from every direction. She did not feel alone anymore, not with ten other girls in her room. She left with her newfound treasures, ready for a serious cleanup and change of clothing. Will life be really great from now on? Will everyone be nice to her? The young man at the door she hadn't noticed before insisted on carrying her luggage to her room. He called himself Bela.

12

Erika came out of the gloomy hallway into the bright courtyard. The morning sun had already melted muddy patches on the hard gravel, and old snow hid in dirty piles against the walls. She had to raise her hand over her eyes to shield off the sparkling glare of the snowy mountainside above. Like huge icebergs ready to crunch the little village at their feet, tall cliffs towered over the old garrison. She wished she had sunglasses, for at least the first few minutes she was completely snow blind.

The late November day began to turn unseasonably warm, turning low lying pastures into a pale green carpet, like there had been a very short winter already and it was time to grow again. Only the ice-covered mountains hugging the small valley proved that it was winter in Tirol. The light rain the day before was long gone. It washed the valley green and the night frost brushed the new grass into shag.

Erika came to look for Bela. He had to be with the single guys, somewhere at the other side of the compound.

Eddy seemed to have disappeared from the face of the earth, she thought, no one seemed to know about him. Is Bela on the same track? Are boys so undependable?

She noticed the man in his Red Cross uniform at the top of the landing to the offices. The few minutes of their encounter on the train was far in the past, but his was a face at least she had seen before. He was admiring the beauty of the mountains and did not notice her approach. The little plastic tag pinned to his uniform simply said 'Williams,' she did not recall his first name.

"Good Day," she looked up from the bottom of the stairs, still shielding her eyes from the sun.

"Ah, it's you," Williams shouted with sudden excitement and ran down to meet her. "You still speak English?"

"Yes, little," she said showing a pinch between her fingers.

"Boy, I am sure glad that you do. Everyone speaks German around here, or Hungarian. With all these people in camp we have what you call a communication gap, and our two minor interpreters can't be everywhere. Don't you think?"

"Please," she interrupted, "talk slow for me to understand."

"Oh, I'm sorry. I'll slow down. You just holler when I don't, OK?"

"Holler?"

"Yes, just stop me right in my tracks." He thought the sentence over again and shook his head. This is going to be hard. With his left hand he wiped off the words from an imaginary blackboard and started again. "OK, when I," and he pointed to himself, "talk too fast," he said slowly, "You," and pointed at her," "Say Stop! Too Fast, OK?"

"OK," she smiled.

"Well then, if you recall, I am Ken Williams from Winsted, Connecticut, and I work for the American Red Cross." He saw the puzzled look on her face. "I am from America," and raised his arm to show behind the mountains.

"Yes, I know. My father is in America."

"Oh, then you are an American who was born in Hungary."

"No. My father went to the Russian Front in 19-44," She was proud to remember that the year in America should be said like that. Nineteen-fortyfour, not like onethousand-ninehundred-fortyfour in Hungary. "He never came home from war. He went to America."

"So that is why you wanted to learn English. You are going to see him. Where is he in America?"

"Do not know. We never had letters. But I know he is there, someplace."

"I hope you'll find him. It's a very big place, this America. I forgot your name."

"Molnar Erika."

"Molnar," he amused, "very unusual name for a girl."

"No, no, no," she laughed, "Erika is the girl. Molnar is family name." She made a mental note that in America there are first and last names.

"So glad to see you again, Erika," and he extended his hand. He too had learned already, that Hungarian women do shake hands. She took his, and held it for a second. Only their nervous smiles registered the physical contact between two human beings from the opposite sides of earth; the Hungarian girl, who in reality was not yet sixteen, who, over a very brief time had lost her family, her friends, her home and country; and the college student from the University of Hartford, Connecticut who was trying his best to understand this rare jewel he had just found.

"Chocolate. You must like chocolates," he said, "Come," and led her to their office. Small, everyday things, like chocolate, can stir up old memories.

*   *   *

Ken must have been six or seven, he remembered, when a new teacher came to their school. Running up the stairs at home he skipped every second step, radiating with joy. They lived above the furniture store on Water Street then, the long wooden stairs hugging the side of the building going straight up to heaven, it seemed.

"Ma! Ma!' he shouted through the screen door, "This is Janet, my new friend. The teacher said she can help me practice spelling. She is sure smart, Ma, she can spell policemen and university and stuff."

"Hello Mrs. Williams," Janet said politely, still panting from the climb.

"Nice to meet you Janet, come right in." She opened the screen door. "Chocolate. You must like chocolates."

Janet moved to Florida the following year, and mother was taking money now from grocery shoppers way on the other side of the earth. Small, everyday things, like chocolate, can stir up old memories.

*   *   *

Janet might have gone, and Mother will always be in his mind, but Erika is here, standing almost in a daze in the middle of the room. Ken just wanted to touch her pretty face. Instead, he found several bars of chocolate on his boss' desk. He offered the whole box and when the girl took only one, he picked a couple more and handed them to her. "For later, or for a friend," he said. "Do you have any friends here, a boyfriend or something?"

"Everybody is very nice here. All friends. Boys, girls, everybody." She opened her Hershey Bar and took a big bite. Her jaws stopped for a moment and she looked embarrassed. She lifted her hand towards him with anticipation.

"Why not," he said and took a bite. A sweet bite. It was the sweetest chocolate he had ever tasted. The phone rang and she walked out still savoring her Hershey Bar. But only one.

When she came out of the office, Bela was carrying a bucket of coal from the shed. She ran through the yard shading her eyes with one hand from the sharp glare of Muttecopf, the nearest alpine peak she knew by name. Erika felt grateful to those who provided her with food, shelter and clothing, but she could die for a pair of sunglasses.

Bela was glad to see her too. He dropped the bucket and hugged her with familiar ease. "I thought you had gone to America already," he smiled.

"I did not hear of anyone leaving the camp at all," she said. "As a matter of fact, I am still here."

She automatically walked with him towards the men's building, listening to his account of the past few days. How he and some of his friends went to the small town of Warben and found it so much different from the villages back home. "You should see those narrow streets," he exclaimed. "Autos can hardly pass each other. We saw a bus turning a corner, I wouldn't dare put my finger on that wall."

They reached the door to one of the single's room. He put down the bucket again. "Say, why don't we go to town and I'll show you around?"

It sounded like a good idea, something different to do. It was past ten in the morning, she wouldn't even mind missing lunch for a good walk in town. "All right, I'll meet you at the gate in a few minutes, I'll grab a jacket."

In their room Blackie was sitting on her mattress and leaning against the wall, smoking. At her feet, a man in his late twenties rested his hands on his knees, his long legs pulled under him. Erika stood there puzzled when her roommate spoke up.

"Come, just barge right in. We are not doing anything, yet," she winked. "This is Tibor," she pointed at her companion, "he is an actor from the Pest Theater, and he speaks Shakespearian English."

"Really? That's fantastic." She had never met an actor face to face. Only seldom could she afford theater tickets, and her seat was never closer to the stage than the third balcony.

"Erika is a growing young lady," Blackie explained to Tibor. "Much younger than she looks, so watch your mouth."

Tibor was standing now and did not speak for several seconds. Then his deep, clear voice filled the room. "I do not let my eyes be deceived by your beauty; for the aura surrounding you warns off the seductive suggestions my brain is filled with at this moment. Your innocence won the first round over my wickedness, but beware, the flesh is weaker than the soul, and I'll be standing alert to find an appropriate time to gain victory. My pleasure." He extended both of his arms for a handshake.

"Over my dead body. You are mine," Blackie interrupted. "Don't let all that fancy talk fool you. I have been after his body for more than half an hour, but he is too chicken to start anything. Someone may walk in on us, he says."

"I guess he is right," Erika said still clutching the

warmth of Tibor's hands in her palm. His sophistication did make a deep impression on her, and Blackie's charming elocution somewhat confused her. "I am going to town with a friend," she finally said, suddenly, remembering that Bela was waiting. "Do you two care to join us?"

"Are we allowed to leave the camp?" Blackie was concerned.

"Naturally," Tibor assured them. "We are in a free country now, why would anyone stop us?"

The long, narrow country road began at the stone wall of the camp and followed the low rail fence towards the small town about five minutes away. Every now and then, the path made a sharp turn, zigzagging on the bottom of the valley between the towering rocky mountains. They could see the church steeple in the distance surrounded by small stone houses like scared sheep flocked together in the corner of their corral. Once they reached the first house with the country far behind them, they found themselves in a tiny city. The small streets were neatly cleared of snow to let cobblestones show through. Around the center plaza, narrow sidewalks led to neat little shops. They enjoyed the packed windows of the grocery store, the tastefully arranged winter fashions of small boutiques, the elegant white clothed dinner tables of the restaurant. An abundance of merchandise, impeccable cleanliness and fresh mountain air surrounded them in this pleasant new world.

"Look, look! Oranges!" Erika shouted a little too loud. "So many and they are huge." They looked at the mounds of fruit in admiration, like they had just discovered a famous painting for the first time. The neat rows of perfect spheres were pyramiding over almost half of the window space, sharing the rest with bananas, figs and a large heap of brown roasted coffee beans.

"I do not want to seem extravagant," Tibor announced, "but may I be permitted to treat us with one of those delicacies." He juggled some coins in his pocket and waited for a reaction.

"Man, don't let us spoil your fun," Bela said impatiently. "Just make it quick."

Tibor entered the store and they followed him in. They didn't want to miss the occasion to explore the inside of the place. The tiny bell still echoed as they approached the glass counter of the delicatessen. The aroma of fresh fruit, strange spices and silk candy filled their nostrils. Their eyes were hungrily taking in not only the countless variety of the items, but also the abundance of each. Shelves full of different chocolate bars in their fancy wrappings fit right in with the bins of peanuts, Saint John's Bread and hazelnuts. Erika felt that it was not such a good idea after all to come in here; the smells and sights made her hungry.

"*Ein orange bitte.*" Tibor smiled lifting his index finger to the salesgirl behind the counter. She smiled back understandingly, and motioned him to make his own selection. After the transaction was concluded and the deal was closed with the ringing of the register, Tibor escorted his companions to the sidewalk. Delicately balancing the orange on three fingers of his left hand, he stretched out his right palm. "Now, if someone would lend me a pocketknife, I will demonstrate how to properly consume this gem."

Bela opened his knife and landed it on Tibor's palm like it was a surgical tool. They all concentrated their attention on the expert movement as he made a shallow incision in the skin of the fruit cutting a perfect circle, gently, so as not to break the inner membranes holding in the juices. He continued to make a similar cut ninety degrees away, and two more to end up with eight flawlessly even sections of the skin. A small circle around the navel ended the operation. He closed and returned the knife. With two fingers he gently lifted out the navel and peeled each section beginning at the top and stopping just before the breaking point at the bottom. After long, agonizing minutes the fruit resembled a pretty orange colored flower with a huge yellow center.

There were eleven slices in that orange. Although Tibor had paid for it, he generously took one less than the rest. They walked down on the sunny side of the sidewalk, savoring it slowly so as not to miss even a drop of the juice, hanging on to this new taste as long as they could. When all was gone, Tibor came out with another item from his vast expertise in the citrus field. He took a piece of orange peel between his fingers and broke it quickly with a snap. From the sudden pressure, juice squirted out of the rind straight into Erika's face. She laughed and returned the attack. They all joined in, trying to make as many breaks on the rinds as possible. After the short battle was over, they learned that the soft inner part of the skin was also edible.

"I have heard that if you place these skins on the top of the stove," someone commented, "a nice aroma will fill the room."

"It's the oil that evaporates," Tibor announced expertly.

Suddenly the cityscape ended and they found themselves in the country again. The road in the distance disappeared like it was swallowed up by Muttecopf.

"They say that mountain there is 2777 meters high," Bela announced. "Let's climb it."

"You think we can?" Blackie worried.

A small pine forest bordered the foot of the mountain, and the road they followed made a turn into it.

At closer range, the mountain did not look so high anymore, and once inside the forest it lost its effect completely. A tiny brook appeared on the side of the road, and as they walked, the boys made small snowballs to practice target shooting on distant tree trunks.

The slight gradual increase in altitude went unnoticed until at a sharp bend of the road, they realized the brook was gone and a deep ravine had taken its place. They must have walked a few hours without feeling tired, enjoying the fresh crisp mountain air. At one point, anther brook came up to the road, or perhaps it was the same one. By this time its surface was covered with a layer of thin ice, following the contour of boulders and small rocks with little waterfalls between them. Like a freshly plowed ice garden, the stream came out of the woods with unequalled beauty. Bela took a small rock and cracked a hole on the top of one of the tiny icebergs. Water gushed out in short squirts as the brook splashed between the rocks underneath. He tasted nature's most unique water cooler and found it refreshing.

"Look, a deer," Erika whispered, covering her mouth. A full-grown doe stood under the pine branches staring right at them, motionless, unafraid. Blackie took several steps towards the animal, leaving the road. The snow under her feet had a supporting frozen crust. The deer watched her closing in, then playfully jumped to disappear in the woods. A short distance away the trees thinned into a clearing to expose a large open field. A slight slant upwards toward the horizon ended in a sharp even line.

"It looks like the top of the mountain," Bela mused. "I bet if we walked up there, we'd find our camp right below our feet." They also speculated that the day was getting late and they would save a lot of walking by completing the circle downhill to Warben. The surface of the snow held on strong, and pretty soon they were out in open terrain disturbed occasionally by boulders, some as large as a village house.

Tibor was the first to notice the small footprints of hunting dogs on the snow, or perhaps they were getting close to a farm. But Bela, who spent his early boyhood in the country, took a closer look at the marks. If they were really from dogs, where were the hunter's footprints, he reasoned. He motioned Tibor to the side, out of earshot of the girls.

"I don't think this is right," pointing to the prints getting more numerous.

"What do they appear to you?" Tibor asked with some concern.

"I hope I'm wrong, but they could be wolves'."

"Don't fuck with me man, this is serious." He suddenly lost his sophistication and cultured manner. Fright turned his smooth face to pale yellow. His eyes grew visibly smaller as he glanced around, not too slowly, hoping that by not seeing, he would not find anything there. In the far corner to the right, he did notice a large boulder void of any trees or vegetation. Without a word, the two men headed for it. It was still good daylight, and the tracks they followed so far obviously continued in the direction of the rock, disappearing in a ditch at the bottom of the boulder. A slight breeze came in toward them and they suddenly picked up the unmistakable stench of wolves.

While he was younger than his partner, Bela quickly took charge of the situation. He was carrying a small pine branch as a walking stick he had cleared earlier with his pocketknife. A stick and a knife made up the whole arsenal of weapons they possessed. If they got any closer to the den, or the wind changed direction, he knew they would be defenseless even against a single animal, let alone a pack. At first he stopped the girls from getting any closer. Then, in a whisper, he explained that they were heading in the wrong direction and the day was getting old too. The best thing was, he suggested, to turn around and head back to camp the same way they came.

Blackie got suspicious first. "Why the whisper? Only God can hear us up here," she shouted towards the sky. "Besides, we are almost at the top, aren't we?"

"No, we can not go any further, we must turn around," Tibor chimed in nervously.

"There is something up there, isn't there?" Blackie gasped. "You saw something up there, you just don't want to tell us."

"We better go now, before it is too late," said Bela, forcing the girls to turn.

Blackie stopped and turned again towards the mountaintop, looking over Bela's shoulder, searching for something to see. "Too late for what? For Christ's sake, what are you two talking about?"

"God damnit, girls! There are wolves up there!" Tibor lost his nerve again, "let's get the hell out of here."

The last remark seemed needless, for both girls jumped to a fast sprint down the hill, holding their hands to their mouths to stop them from screaming. There was no need for further explanation, the situation was well understood. They also realized that no one in the refugee camp knew about their mountain trip; hardly anyone knew their names in the camp, or that they had left their home country at all. They were not registered anywhere, and if lost up here, there would be no one ever to search for them.

Mere panic slowly increased their speed of descent. With that, their weight grew above the endurance of the thin ice under their feet. Tibor, being the heaviest, broke through first. His knee disappeared in the snow and with a sudden jerk, his other leg followed. Bela tried to stop and come to the aid of his friend, but he fell and broke the ice with his elbows. Until then, they had not realized that they were walking on top of snow whose depth they did not dare imagine.

Their instincts directed them towards the nearest wooded area. All four fell several times before they reached the first tree, helping each other out of the sharp holes their feet made in the ice, struggling soundlessly, throwing frightful glances back to the top of the mountain. Inside the forest it turned considerably darker. They knew that they must find the road, any road; in a very short time before they got hopelessly lost in the woods that began to get less and less familiar.

Vague sounds of a distant church bell made them change direction in the snowy thicket. When the darkness of evening began to close in on them, a trickle of faint light came through where the trees thinned out. Behind it, at quite a distance, was the village of Warben.

13

The man in his late sixties was short, chubby and wore the distinguished red round face of a typical Austrian merchant. He walked in brisk, short steps, much too fast for his age, but sturdy and youthful, acquired by decades of climbing the steep mountain streets of Tirol. At this time, he was agitated and angry, for he was in search of his thieves.

He came to the Hungarian refugee camp accompanied by a policeman from Imst, the nearest mountain town where the valleys of Obertal and Pitztal meet in a small plateau, the only community in the area large enough to have a police force. The village of Warben accepted the more than 200 homeless refugees with compassion and with the excitement of being inherently close to these fierce political events.

The old man was among the first to open his heart and bankbook to come to the aid of the needy. Today he went another step further when he found a young couple strolling downtown. He observed at first, how hungrily they looked at the well-stocked window of the food market; he saw the thrill in their eyes at the sight of all the hanging slabs of smoked meat, shelves of crusty bread and mounds of tropical fruit glimmering through the frosty glass. He wanted to invite them to a nice restaurant meal. He could not speak to them, but his friendly eyes and disarming smile convinced the young man and his companion that the gentle tap on the shoulder and the waving of the arm meant something good.

They followed him into the interior of a small establishment and sat timidly on the wooden chairs around a large table covered with white damask. Behind them, hanging on the sparkling stucco, a huge wall decoration made from tips of skis formed the petals of an Edelweiss. A waiter came shortly and brought fresh brown bread and butter to the table, following it with a tureen of hot soup. Soon their dinner arrived without ever ordering it. The trio went through the silent meal smiling and glancing at each other occasionally with mutual appreciation. The girl giggled sheepishly and spoke to her friend a few times, but the old man just smiled, for he knew that he had made them happy.

After the hearty meal, pitchers of strong alpine beer arrived and were readily consumed by the men. The girl sipped slowly only a glassful throughout the afternoon. By the time darkness fell on the town, the old man, from the cold, the heavy meal and the large amount of beer, fell asleep at the table. When he awoke, he told police, the couple he treated was gone and so was his wallet. He did not say how much money was missing; he only wanted its return.

The word that some refugees stole money from a helpful Austrian spread quickly through the camp. The security force, set up by the Hungarians themselves, was busy keeping the upset masses from tearing at each other with shameful accusations. The Hungarian camp Commandant and the head of the security squad accompanied the Austrians going from room to room and floor to floor in search of the young couple.

Erika was in her room when the delegation arrived, and while she did not understand the commotion, the shaking finger pointing at her sent shivers down her back. The smile of the kind gentleman was gone now, only the red face got redder, shouting angry foreign words at her. It took extra guards to remove her from the room to the safety of the police station, while the search went on for her companion.

"I can't believe she did it," said Ken to the Commandant when he learned what happened. He was involved with something at the office at the time and didn't even want to interfere in the proceedings. It was not a Red Cross affair, not until it did become the affair of Ken Williams. He had spent many hours lately with Erika in his spare time, helping her read English and build her vocabulary. In a very short time, he grew from a helpful tutor to a caring mentor. Now he felt he was more than that. He rushed to the police station.

Erika recounted the day's events to the Hungarian Commandant, step by step, even to the details of their menu. She did not recall any part of the alleged crime. When she had come back from the ladies room, the Austrian gentlemen's face rested on the tablecloth, his supportive arms across the front of it. Bela seemed to be in much better shape, leaning back in his chair with his feet stretched out under the table. He did act agitated, scorned her for spending too much time in the lavatory, and insisted on leaving in a hurry. She did not see any wallet, nor did she know who paid the tab.

Ken was also interested in knowing, if perhaps the restaurant staff was responsible for the theft. It was at this time that police brought Bela in. He was swearing loudly at Erika for turning him in, although she wasn't even there when the old Austrian identified him. He swore at the refugee system for not providing enough financial aid, which forced him to steal, and swore at the Russians for forcing him into this situation.

Erika was eventually cleared of any wrongdoing; the Commandant apologized to the merchant and to the police and escorted Erika home. Calming the rest of the refugees was another matter.

"We have to get you out of here as soon as possible," Ken suggested and the Commandant approved. Peter Varga's arrival at the office just then was a pleasant surprise.

"I just heard what happened. She's only a young girl, incapable of doing such a thing. I vouch for her." He spoke fast but calmly. A resolution had to be made in a hurry.

"We could send her to Bergau," the Commandant said finally. "But they take families only. She is alone."

"I can take her as family," Peter said firmly. "My wife and I can claim her as a sister or niece, would that be possible?"

Erika became agitated. "If I did not do it why can't I stay? I have friends here now. I don't want to go."

"You can't explain your innocence to every person in the Lager," the Commandant said. "In the meantime you are in extreme danger. I think Peter's idea is best"

Ken offered to let her stay in his office until the morning transport arrived. Peter volunteered to gather her belongings from her room. For the time being, being in custody explained her absence.

Early next morning three other families accompanied Peter and his new family on the few hour trip to their new lodging. The small mountain bus labored up the steep hill. The sun was shining but could not attack the thin layer of packed snow on the pavement. They had left the Inn River valley a short time ago, heading up to the upper levels of the gorgeous Alps. The curvy, treacherous road raised them to an altitude of at least a half-kilometer before they found themselves in another valley filled with the dark blue waters of the Bergensee. Narrow and long, disappearing in the distance, the mountain lake sparkled in the afternoon sun. Rich travelers from the West would have paid a good sum for a scenic ride like this, the refugees paid for it by giving up their homeland. At the next turn of the narrow road the village of Bergau emerged. Typical of Alpine communities, a row of Tirolean style houses flanked the two sides of the only street. Their wooden facades and hand carved decorative balconies accented the simple lives of the mountain men. The roofs, already covered with a thin layer of snow, were braced with large rocks spread out at random to protect their owners from sudden avalanches covering their front doors.

They advanced slowly through town, past the only church and a few commercial buildings. Small children waved at the bus; the refugees returned the gesture; curious adults looked on suspiciously. Winter had not officially begun yet; the ski season was starving for more snow. Mother Nature declined. The days were comfortably warm, and cool nights protected the light white blanket at the foot of the mountains.

"I read somewhere," Peter informed his fellow passengers, "that these mountain lakes can be as much as 200 meters deep. Just imagine," he pointed straight at the steep rocky slopes on both sides of the water ahead of them. "They go straight down to meet in the middle. Water just keeps filling up the gap in between." Tourist boats travel up and down the length of the narrow waters, but by this time of the year, icing required the captains to pull all the vessels out to safe storage. The younger generation, on the other hand, were impatiently waiting for cold to start the skating season.

A large, white, three-story building appeared in the distance. Its proximity to the beach area suggested it was a hotel. When the bus pulled into the spacious driveway, only a small sign, Gasthous, above the front entrance revealed their destination. A large, friendly man in dark green Tirolean folksuit greeted them at the door.

Their earlier refuge was primitive compared to the apparent luxury of their new residence. Peter led the way to their assigned room on the second floor. Two large beds with modern mattresses, and not bundled up straw, a bureau and some chairs were all the furnishings. But there was a private bathroom with a shower and even a bidet. The meager belongings of the new family did not take up too much space. Edit Varga could not curtail her excitement.

"This is great, just great," she said over and over again. "What a Christmas present."

The holidays were just around the corner, less than a week away. It would be their first ever, away from their families and friends, away from home in a foreign land with an unfamiliar language, in beautiful but still strange surroundings. Even if Christmas was not a big issue in their lives, the birth of Christ began to form a different meaning. The communist government could not eradicate the religious customs of their society, so they cleverly renamed the day to the Holiday of the Pine and placed more emphasis on New Year's Eve celebration. Still, under the cliffs of the Alps, Hungarians had this jittery feeling of being detached from their old life and not yet accepted in the new.

Edit pushed her husband into the bathroom and closed the door. "How long is this kid staying with us? We have not had a private moment since we left Hungary," she scolded.

"Exactly that. She is only a kid. What were you expecting me to do? She was in trouble and now she needs us."

"Of course, Darling. I am just longing for you," she rubbed against him. "Please try something to get rid of her."

Edit opened the door and proceeded to dictate arrangements. Erika got the bed near the entrance of the room, the couple the one next to the window and the pretty view. Edit assigned a drawer for Erika's belongings and asked her to shove her suitcase under her bed. Moving day was over.

The hotel had eighteen rooms already occupied by refugee families, most with small children. With the newcomers arrival there were no more vacancies. There were no Commandants and security squads here; the owner and his wife were all the authority there was. The poor ski season forced the couple to turn to the Red Cross. The $2 a day per person stipend and all the raw materials to feed them came to a good deal, considering that full occupancy ensured a better profit than any good ski season could ever provide. In addition, all the hotel staff was laid off except for a cook. Refugees were assigned on a daily basis to work in the kitchen and serving, cleaning the halls and the common bathrooms, and of course, taking care of the linen. It did not matter; the refugees felt useful and it occupied their abundant free time; the owners' good-hearted charity turned a profit too.

The days were spent acclimating to their new surroundings, sprucing up their residences, eating well three times a day at the hotel's restaurant and taking luxurious baths. Acquaintances turned to friendships, some even graduated to romance. Erika had a hard time finding someone close to her age and had to spend long periods with her adopted family.

It was Peter's idea to get a Christmas tree. They left the hotel one bright sunny morning and turned toward the mountainside. Millions of pine trees of all sizes surrounded them. And yet it took several hours to find just the right specimen, a silver pine, not taller than a bouquet of flowers, perfectly shaped. It felt criminal to cut down such a young plant, but in compensation Edit carried it home in her arms like it was a baby. Peter carved a tiny cross for its base and they began to search their belongings to find things to use for decorations. It was at just this time that the group was summoned to the lobby for a meeting.

The hotel owner expressed his joy in sharing the holidays with his large, extended family, pointed out the beautifully decorated floor to ceiling pine in the corner of the room as his personal present to them, and opened a large cardboard box in the middle of the room. He began to read the accompanying Christmas card to a translator.

"*Frohe Weihnachten und ein gluckliches newes Jahr.*" The short holiday greeting card was signed by about a dozen schoolchildren from Germany. From the box large bars of Swiss chocolate appeared; a line was formed and the presenting began. It took several trips to the box until it was empty.

"This is an armful," Erika gasped, "We don't need any other food for a week." A small bag of Hershey Kisses was among their presents and it worked just great as decorations for their own small tree. A few pretty gift box ribbons were also found and were ripped to shreds to complete the trimming of the tiny work of art. Erika never had such a beautiful Christmas tree in her life, or any Christmas tree at all.

The big day finally came with all its pomp and warmth. The dining room was decorated with pine twigs and ribbons; the festive meal accented the occasion. Turkey was not a common food in Hungary and came as a real treat. A large orange rested next to everyone's plate for dessert.

Edit suggested they attend midnight Mass. It seemed winter had the same idea; a light snow began to fall from the dark sky. Walking to the church in solemn silence was a deep part of a new religious experience as they watched the lighted steeple of the church searching for heaven. On the balcony near the top a lone man appeared. The thrilling notes of Silent Night flowed from his trumpet; the compelling sounds reverberated from the mountainsides, bouncing back and forth towards the outer end of the valley in multiple echoes. After the first stanza another trumpeter joined in, then another and another aiming at all four sides of the universe. The grandest, most acclaimed symphony in the world could not surpass this uplifting message from the Creator. The music enticed more and more refugees to make the short stroll, to sit on the low stone walls guarding the churchyard. Some did not even want to enter the church; if there was a forgiving God up there, he was with them here, under the falling snow.

The week between the holidays went quietly. Erika wished she had a good book to read, or any book for that matter. She stayed in their room for hours and kept busy with her English notes. It was sad that Ken was not there, but she cherished the many words he wrote down for her to learn. Wouldn't it be nice if she knew enough to write a letter to him, but she didn't even know his address. The knock on the door broke her reverie, but when she answered, she knew that now she was really dreaming.

"Merry Christmas," Ken said in a deep voice.

She stood there at the open door ready to faint. Was her wish this powerful? She also wished to know what to do next.

"Cat caught your tongue?" he asked closing the do
or behind him. A tiny green box tied with a ribbon

was in his outstretched hand. Finally, she gently pushed the gift aside, and hugged him with both arms. Her face lay on his chest, his arms encircling her back. For a few seconds they stood there in compressed happiness. That was all they wanted to do.

"Thank you," she said quietly.

"Thank you!" putting his gift in her palm.

"I was dreaming about you."

"Really? When?"

"Just now, before you came."

"You should have sweet dreams," he smiled, waiting for her to open the box.

"I only have sweet dreams." She untied the small ribbon, like she would use it again for something. They did not wrap gifts in Hungary, not even Christmas presents. They trimmed their trees, those who still practiced the custom, on the eve of the holiday. Children went to bed early that evening and stayed awake half the night in anticipation. The Angel brought their gifts, and laid them on the floor around the tree. When morning came, a few toys, some socks and sweaters, or even a pair of new pajamas made up the great festivity. Erika never even had that much. The colorful little ribbon she folded and placed on the table. She opened the box ceremoniously to reveal a dainty silver necklace tied to a gorgeous Edelweiss. She smiled again longingly, but did not touch it.

"May I?" Ken asked as he opened the clasp. She turned her back to him, waiting.

"I have nothing for you," she said standing in front of the mirror on the wall. She admired it, in the mirror first, then lifting it in her palm, she gently kissed it.

"Sure you do, I am looking at her."

She moved to him and gave a pecking kiss on his face. He turned his other side and pointed. She giggled and kissed again.

"You missed a spot in between," Ken dared. She dared to. Both blushed as they plopped down on her bed.

"How did you get here?" she asked finally.

"Oh, I got How Do You Do's car."

"You call him that too?"

"No, I never do, but I think he knows about it. It's kind of cute. So, here I am, I had to see you on the holidays, and," he took a long pause, "it was official too. I have a letter to deliver." From his pocket he pulled out a small envelope simply addressed to 'Erika.' "This guy is sending it to you. Eddy or something." He did not dwell on the details much; just that her former boyfriend was sent to another camp, an all male camp to be sure. She stood up and placed the mail next to the ribbon.

"It's almost lunchtime, are you hungry?" She felt she had no right to offer the hotel's food, but Ken was with the Red Cross so it must be all right.

"You would like to go somewhere? We have a car."

She wanted to stay there, right in her room, to not share him with anyone or anything. But what if the other tenants of the room came back? What if she wanted to kiss him more and he would demure? What if nothing would happen?

She chose their dining room. The food was simple but followed Hungarian cuisine and taste. The refugees took turns preparing and serving under the supervision of the hotel's cook. She did make faces at the amounts of garlic and paprika they used, but it all worked out fine.

During their short meal, Ken told all the latest news of her old camp; that it was to be closed down in the middle of next month; where they all were going to move, and also how much he missed her and how strange his first Christmas was alone. He promised to find her a place at the new camp. No one would remember the shameful incident so long ago, he assured her. Erika listened intently and played with her food. They walked out of the hotel unnoticed.

"What a gorgeous view," Ken commented taking in the lake. "Too bad we can't swim now."

"Can't ski either," she joked.

They strolled down to the small pier, arm in arm, pretending they might slip on the wet snow.

"My gosh!" he said looking at his watch. "It's time for me to leave."

At the car he kissed her again in the same order as she did before. She had to tiptoe to return his farewell. She quickly turned and ran into the hotel. She did not want to see him departing, nor to let him see her tears.

"See you in a couple of weeks!" he shouted as the Volkswagen chugged away.

Coming to her senses, Erika ran to the kitchen. She had nearly forgotten her cleanup assignment. She suppressed her feelings dipping into the dishwater; the longing for him, the memory of their brief romantic episode, the scent of his shaving lotion, and the sudden miracle of how it all happened. But the pretty jewel dangling under her chin reminded her she had to tolerate the next few weeks without him.

After the kitchen was properly cleaned, the crew parted and she walked up to her room still in a daze. The Vargas were not home yet and she stretched out on the top of her bed, arms beneath her neck. Then she remembered the letter. She reached over the table with a lot of hesitation in the process. Should she read it at all? Who is he to her now? Disappearing into thin air, then bothering her like this? She tapped the envelope on her fingers. The lone word, Erika, bounced rhythmically in the air. 'He has neat handwriting," she thought and opened it.

Erika Dear!

I have stayed away from you all these days with pain in my heart. You see I knew you belonged to him, the one on the border. I wanted to give you time to forget him, but now you have disappeared! Where are you???

Now they are taking me someplace. Are we ever to meet again? Are you happy? Because I am miserable and lonely. Look for me in America.

Oh, Erika Dear, do whisper in my ear that you love me....!

Eddy

Just that. Short and simple, like you can look through America from one end to the other. Like she would know his last name at least. 'Eddy, Eddy,' she sighed, clutching the letter to her breast. 'We met at the wrong time, at the very wrong time! Maybe if Ken wasn't here, maybe in another life.' She tore up the letter.

Sylvester Night came just as fast; the anticipated New Year's Eve revelry had always been the highlight of the year in Hungary. This time, Old Man 1956 would finally be driven away by 1957's mysterious little kid in diapers witnessed by family and friends who gathered to celebrate life with zest, burying their troubles with food, music and wine.

The hotel did not disappoint its guests. The main hall was filled with long decorated tables; a small local band moved people to the dance floor, and even beer was provided. Villagers were invited also to mingle with the

Hungarians and a lot of smiles and gestures complemented conversation. If only remorse didn't interfere with their joy, but there were things painfully missing. The familiar surroundings of home, the gypsy music, the sometimes off key chorus of folklore sung after a few cheers of Tokay wine; and yes, even the traditional stuffed cabbage was missing. Sometimes being ungrateful can be a cardinal sin, and sometimes it's just unavoidable.

Erika did not want to repeat the misery drinking beer could bring. Peter offered her a Coca Cola with a warning. "Now, be careful. This stuff is known not only to induce imperialist thinking, but also intoxication. We were warned against it for years."

"You are joking, yes?"

"Not at all. It was part of our communist curriculum in Political Science. Coke is derived from narcotics and could be addictive. So take it easy."

She smirked and took a big gulp. It was lukewarm, bubbly and strange, but it was not unpleasant. She danced a little with Peter and also with a young Austrian. The evening just flew away while she finished a second bottle of Coke.

Midnight came and was celebrated with loud cheers and singing, first their national anthem, then traditional Christmas tunes about the Angel's gifts and a new baby in the middle of the desert. Erika's eyelids grew heavy and she excused herself.

"Shit," she mumbled staggering up the stairs. "Peter was right, I must be drunk." She giggled and fumbled to find the doorknob, and without turning on the light she stretched out on her bed.

"Not a bad start for a new year, heh?" she asked the ceiling. While waiting for an answer, she fell asleep.

14

When Erika woke the sun was reflecting off the lower valley but she did not know what time it was. The bed next to hers was empty; only faint noises came from the bathroom. They must be in there, Peter and Edit, she thought, and looked at the ceiling smiling. She felt no hangover or anything, but how would she know, she had never been drunk before, ever. And how was it last night? How silly she must have been acting on the presumed affects of Coca Cola? She looked the ceiling again. No, she felt that way because she wanted to feel like an adult. Children don't get drunk, only sick, and she felt good feeling like an adult.

Edit came out of the bath. "Oh, you are up. I'm scheduled to work lunch and I'm late. Would you please clean up in there for me?" She left the room. Peter must be down at the dining room already, Erika thought. Couples were usually assigned together.

She filled the tub and dug through her new wardrobe for something to wear. The warm water felt good. Alone and free, she became conscious of her body, searching for flaws, some things that she might outgrow, others that would worsen with age. Not bad, she thought; nice light skin, firm calves that could be emphasized by high heels, if she ever owned any. And why not, she mused, I am in a new world full of opportunities. "What a great life," she announced loudly to the mirror after drying herself. She tossed the towel on the chair in the back just as the bathroom door opened slowly. An all-smiling Peter stood there totally naked. His protruding erection came closer with every step.

Erika stood there frozen. No screams came, no sudden jumps for cover, just a petrified attempt to avoid looking at him. Her hands instinctively covered her pubic area, bending down in hopeless protection.

"What gorgeous tits at such a young age," Peter said leaning his arm against the wall. Erika cupped her breasts in desperation.

"Now, that is even better. The triangle of bliss that men so insanely covet. Am I scaring you?"

"Yes," she muttered, "Yes, yes!" Her weak voice sounded like a premature orgasm.

"You dirty slut! You stinking whore! So this is what you were after?" Edit screamed from the doorway. "Get the fuck out of our lives! Do it fast before I find something to kill you with."

Now it was Peter's turn to cover himself as Erika zoomed by. He desperately searched for a quick explanation. "I couldn't help it, honest," he said, his manhood lame, reaching nervously for Erika's towel.

The bathroom door closed behind Erika. Muffled voices she could not make out followed her as she dressed and packed her little suitcase.

"Ok, she seduced you," Edit said. "I knew this would happen, I told you before. I don't blame you for your weakness, and thank God, the Temptress is now out of here,"

"I am going with her," Peter said quietly.

"You're what?" Edit screamed again. "Break up our marriage for a filthy fling?"

"We are not married, and you know it. You would have lost me to a singles quarters if we didn't make this up. So, shut up and go back to work."

"Peter, don't do this to me, to us. If you must, go get her out of your system, but come back to me. She is out there spread-eagled on our bed, ready for you." But the room was empty.

Erika ran down the stairs, never noticing anyone she passed, her tears silently washing her red face. The ugly, shocking scene was behind her. Through the decorative front door of the hotel, a pleasant new world embraced her. The calm waters of the lake caressed the sandy shores with small strokes. The sky came down to share its ozone with the soothing scent of giant pines. She ran and walked in spurts, ignoring it all.

"All men are devils from hell, ugly, heartless bastards!" She talked out loud like a senile old maid. She will, she promised herself, stay an old maid and wait for senility. There are no good men, she concluded, not in her life anyway. Except her grandfather. He was a good man and he had to die for it. And Frank too, and he had to die. Maybe Ken, the American. He was good to her, and she would see him soon, but where? Her hurts and sorrows kept popping back from her past, too fresh to be diluted by time. At the fork of the road she stopped in confusion.

The town was behind her now and the desolate tracks were leading to places with strange names. Fugen came in weakly in her memory. It seemed to her that there was another refugee camp there, even if it was 12 kilometers away, it was worth the try. She picked up her pace with renewed ambition. Being sad, lonely and ashamed could wait. The ever-present pine forest closed in on her as the pavement began to rise again. She did not pay attention to the gray van passing her.

The vehicle stopped in the middle of the road and backed towards her. A young man rolled down the passenger window. *"Wohin sie, bitte, Frauline?"* and he smiled. The words did not register with her, but she knew shaking her head sent an international message. Whatever they wanted, she was not interested and kept on walking.

The van stayed with her. Long dialogues in foreign tongue were exchanged inside; sneering and teenage horselaughs amused the occupants. Erika knew that there must be at least two people in there. They sped up suddenly and pulled in front of her. Two youngsters stepped out and leaned their backs on the rear of the vehicle, their arms folded. Waiting.

She dropped her luggage and looked around. Not a soul in sight. Only the snowy road in front and behind her. The forest enveloped the rest. The boys approached her calmly on either side, grabbing her before she let out the first scream. She did not realize she could cry out for help only in Hungarian. But she repeated it again and again. The boys opened the back door of the van with their free hands and shoved her inside. The floor of the compartment was layered with several horse blankets, a ready-made bed on wheels. The young men jumped in and slammed the door shut. One climbed towards the front and plopped down facing the action. He grabbed her upper body and pulled her closer to his lap. The other worked feverishly to loosen her lower garments. The first ripped her blouse open and grabbed her breasts. The second labored on his own pants. She kept screaming.

The rear door of the van burst open. A very large somebody seized the legs of the nearest attacker and flung him with such force he helplessly tumbled several times in the air before landing with a screaming thump. Now he cradled

Erika as gently as he could and lifted her out of the van only seconds before it moved away. The boy jumped up from the ditch and ran desperately after it.

Erika stood in a daze. Shaking all over, she hardly could find the buttons to straighten her clothes. She looked at the giant standing there smiling, his arms moving back and forth like a small child showing his deed for approval. He was at least two meters tall, husky to make the balance, and not more than twenty years old.

"I heard your screams," he said shyly looking at his feet. "I guess the whole valley heard it, but they don't understand Hungarian."

"My God, you are Hungarian!"

"With a name Kish, I must be."

"Kish? Like little?" she couldn't hold back a faint smile.

"See? I made up that name deliberately. I am frighteningly huge, but when I introduce myself like that, it breaks the ice. People sometimes even laugh."

"You made up your name? What do they really call you?"

"Imre."

"I get it," she said relaxing a bit, "Imre the Kish is not as frightening as Imre the Huge. But it works."

"Imre is real, Kish is made up. You see, here in this foreign world, some of us have no papers; they were taken away in jail, lost in a battle, or conveniently misplaced. Now we can be anybody we want to be."

"Do you think I did the same thing?" Erika looked at him suspiciously.

"Oh, no. I don't mean that. I don't even know your name, why would I think that?"

"Erika," she said nervously. "You want to know my real family name or the false one?" She felt threatened by the very same person who just saved her. Maybe he saved her for himself? No, she calmed down somewhat, he looked harmless. Besides, he couldn't have known what he was getting into, or what was happening in the van.

"Now, I know you, and you know me," she went on avoiding the question. "What I would like to know is, how did you happen to be here?"

"Well, to make a long story short, from the border I wound up in a small Gasthaus in Pertisau. The owner changed his mind about taking in refugees and we were evicted. Unfortunately, I was roaming around in town when it happened. When I got to our room, everyone was gone. I heard about Bergau, so I walked out there. They told me they take families only. I'm only nineteen, too young to get married, so I walked again looking for a place to stay. I was in the woods, doing my business, when you walked by. The van was right behind you. That's it."

They were standing where she had dropped her luggage. Imre picked it up and they started to walk. "Where are we going?"

"I think it's Fugen, but I am not sure," she said.

"If you think it has a place for us, may I join you?"

The question was more apologetic than silly. Alone in the wilderness, somewhere between two mountain villages, they had no alternative. Walking slowly together in silence for a while was almost natural. She tried hard to brush the past from her mind and concentrate on the present. The young man next to her seemed to glide, taking small steps to match hers.

"Oh, my God," she stopped suddenly, covering her face with her hands. "I didn't even thank you. Oh, please forgive me. Those bastards would have had to kill me first to get their way with me, and I am so ungrateful."

"It happened before," he said calmly returning to the subject. "Rape victims die sometimes before the act. On the way to the gallows, it makes no difference one way or another. Raping, raping and killing, or killing and raping, all come with the same sentence."

"How come you are so expert in punishments and crimes?"

He stopped again and put down the suitcase. He turned towards the mountains rubbing his chin for some time. "All right. Someone must know, and I guess it's better if it's you. I don't know you that well, but I do know what you almost became. So, what I am about to tell you must stay between us. I am the son of the Chief Executioner of Hungary." They moved ahead again.

"Are you serious? Is there such a position? Is there a real person who kills other people, even if it's according to the law? I never thought that it was a civilized thing to do. Was he a hangman?"

"Yes, and still is. He inherited the job from my grandfather; I was next in line."

"That's terrible. Are you that heartless? I can't believe it."

"Heart has nothing to do with it. First, it's mostly criminals who are executed. Somebody has to do it. My family got into it somehow, and there was no way out. At least my father made it to the top. He dealt with some very big heads, excuse the pun. But we lived in a very small village. We were shunned and folks were afraid of us. I never even attended school. What little I know, I learned from my mother. When they needed him, my father got a telegram summoning him for a job. He ate and drank the rest of the time. I was groomed, mentally at least, to be next. Am I boring you or scaring you?"

"No, no. I want to hear this. My God, did you ever have a friend?"

"Not really. In my situation the only thing that helped was my size. You know that people who want to hurt others have to get physical. Get close and throw some punches. But in my age group, nobody dared touch me. So they did the next worst thing. They stayed at a distance, smirked and laughed at me, called me names I did not deserve, all from safely across the street. But it hurt just the same. People always find a way to hurt you."

"So, that's why you are here now, to hide from your past like me."

"You can't have anything to hide from. You are so young, beautiful, and innocent. Perhaps you are just trying to catch up with your parents. In this crazy turmoil, it is a miracle just to find our own selves."

"I am alone," Erika offered her own confession. "My real name is Klein, a Jew. I did not know this until I escaped from Hungary. I was called Molnar before, and thought I was a Catholic. The revolution killed my grandfather and I killed a bunch of Russians in return."

"Whoa!" He just stared at her in disbelief. "You did no such thing."

It was easy now to recall her past in every detail, to balance their confessions to each other, to come clean for once. The giant human to whom she perhaps owed her life, came down to her size; it helped her make peace with the world. All she needed now was shelter, food and some rest. The village they were approaching looked promising. They knew they were in Fugen; the sign at the side of the road said so. The center of town seemed not too far away.

"*Fluchtling lager, bitte,*" she said to a pedestrian, exerting all her knowledge of German. A flow of words, a pointing finger made up the answer. A short distance away it was repeated. The only word stuck out in both occasions was Ebsen. They finally concluded that it must be the name of a town, and that it was thirty kilometers away.

"There is no daylight left to walk that far," Imre commented. He looked around for answers. It came from a triangular road sign with the shape of a steam locomotive on it. "Let's take the train," he suggested and started in the direction of the arrow.

"We have no money, do we?"

He put his arm around her shoulder protectively, the most intimate he dared to be. The station had only a few passengers at this time of the day. Somehow they figured out which direction they had to go to get to Ebsen. The wooden benches around the walls of the hall gave some comfort. They did not recall how long they had to wait before the train arrived and they boarded a second-class coach.

They stayed on the entrance platform, trying to attract as little attention as possible. But the conductor found them.

"*Ungarishe Fluchtling,*" Imre explained. "*Ebsen,*" ending his short speech when he pulled out the inside of his trousers' pocket, the international signal of being penniless. The conductor smiled and closed his change box. "*Verstehen,*" he said, "*Zehn minute,*" and walked away, leaving them the ten minutes of free ride they badly needed.

15

As if to oblige the holiday season, new blankets of snow arrived every other day, sagging pine branches to the limit. The Alps posed their best to heighten merriment. Ken called his mother in America, exchanging cheery wishes to mellow their depressed moods for being so far apart; Mother reassuring her son about his sacrifice for a great cause, son thanking his mother for understanding. But it was difficult to comprehend the mental anguish of the thousands of refugees, facing their first holidays with separation, and the loss of family and friends, some even permanent.

Wynn called his staff to his office for a private greeting and an informative meeting. The news of their camp in Warben closing was not surprising. While the site was acceptable for wartime soldiers, it was very inadequate for civilians, especially children. The lack of a dining facility, proper sanitation and a medical clinic was part of the problem. Lack of developed administrative control was the biggest problem.

"We don't even know who these people are, and there is no system in place to regulate them," the boss explained. "For that matter, we might even be harboring members of the same regime most of these folks are running away from. Just think, the border was open during the first few days of the uprising, anybody could have gotten through, even communists.

Some good news came with the simple announcement that the whole population, refugees and caretakers, were moving to a new location in Ebsen, about a hundred kilometers to the east, but closer to more populated areas. The place could hold over 600 residents, in modern beds and not on top of a pile of straw. It had real showers, a doctor's office and even mail service available. Processing documentation was already in place there and everyone would be provided with an ID card. Moving would begin right after the holidays, and there will be no more new arrivals here.

Ken called his mother again with his new mailing address and to let her know that he was just promoted to the number two position at the new camp. He also learned that there were about 60 such camps in Austria by now, three in the very same town. His was called just Lager-A, but it was the largest in the group, with the most facilities and a huge commercial kitchen.

Wynn traveled in a Volkswagen bug back and forth between the two places, sometimes every day. It turned out to be a major task to prepare to fill one third of the new camp with his own group. Taking over the whole operation was another serious matter. The Red Cross had processed over a hundred thousand refugees by now, he was told from Vienna, and the number could double in no time. The main objective was to gather and move all these people in the shortest time possible. Fortunately, the borders to most civilized countries on the globe were open to provide new homes and new lives for the unfortunates. Representatives of dozens of nations were recruiting their new citizenry at major camps at all times, Ebsen being no exception.

Ken liked his new office, even if it was shared with a Hungarian leader named Andrasy. He spoke reasonably fluent English and perfect German. Registering the multitudes was their major assignment and they were getting along fine. Andrasy was a typical DP. The term of Displaced Person originated at the time when World War II ended, and thousands of people got stranded outside of their homelands. Andrasy declined to return to Hungary, settled down, and married a fine Austrian lady. He also learned to make fancy Tirolean cuckoo clocks; his small shop provided an adequate living. To offer his services to his countrymen, he believed, was his patriotic duty.

Wynn was in a good mood, sipping on 'American' coffee, specially brewed for the 'Yankees' by attentive kitchen people. "I can't believe how they can drink that mud," he commented a few times on local Espresso that was too strong for him and in a tiny glass hardly enough for more than two swallows. "Of course, Europeans don't guzzle coffee all day like we do."

"We are almost moved in," Wynn said, "One more trip to get my own stuff, and I'm done." Ken had made his own move days ago, staying in Ebsen to better control the transition. "Why are they here?" he asked no one in particular, watching the hustle and bustle in the courtyard.

"They ran away from communism," Wynn commented. "They didn't like it, they were in danger, they wanted out."

"I know all that, they didn't like it. All of them? What did they not like? The control? You know, I have been with them for over a month now, I think they need guidance. Most of them cannot decide almost anything for themselves."

"They used to know better before the war," Wynn said. "They had property, religion and the pride of being

Hungarian. Look at that country now. The Russians are back, community this and community that, internationalism that consists of only the Eastern bloc and Moscow. They used to salute each other with the word 'Liberty!' and they didn't even know what it really meant. That's why they are here."

"They had free education and healthcare, almost free lodging and cheap food. They ate at the workplace for almost nothing, for Christ sake, what else could they want?"

"Gee, I did not know that our Political Scientist is so inquisitive and well informed," Wynn smiled. "Our guests are here of their own free will. Maybe a bit disoriented and bitter, but they made it. Now it is our turn to steer them in the right direction." The phone rang and their coffee break was over. Ken stepped out to the veranda to see a strange couple approaching the stairs. A tiny young girl and a very large young boy had just arrived at the camp on foot. He could not believe his eyes when he realized Erika was back in his life again.

Ken had talked to his Mother about Erika; the pleasant but lonely girl, a few years his junior. He thought about her almost daily, wondering if his decision for her to move away was such a good idea. His very brief visit, the happy romantic moments together, he knew he would never forget. He also tried hard to define his position in the girl's life or rather her stand in his. Was she too young and in a fragile mental state to understand his feelings? Were his feelings leaning more towards understanding and caring, and not just a young man's fancy of the opposite sex?

Ken moved, almost running to greet the new arrivals. He made every effort to control his emotions; after all, he was dealing with a teenager, even too young to be out of her country unescorted, and this time they were not alone. He met them at the top of the stairs, his arms automatically reaching out for a hug, but he stopped. "My God, you made it!" he shouted instead. "How did you find this place?"

'I heard your heartbeat,' she wanted to say, but just smiled. She did not want a warmer welcome either. Seeing him so excited made her happy too.

Now Ken focused on Erika's companion. Large seemed to be an understatement. He was tall and burly, contrasted by his young face. He smiled back.

"Two refugees need place," Erika struggled with her English, the first words she had uttered since Ken's visit. But she knew that more words would come, perhaps in a more proper order, now that her mentor, the handsome American was here.

"Come and we'll see," Ken put his arm on Erika's shoulder walking slowly back to his office. "Who is your friend?"

"You my friend, Ken Williams from America. Other friend is Imre. We meet on road. He help me good in trouble."

"Are you in trouble?" It was more important now than greeting Imre. Fortunately Andrasy was also in the room and he converted the story into understandable format.

"Are you hungry, are you well? Let's stop at the kitchen and get you something. In the meantime, Andrasy will find some beds for you somewhere, won't you Commandant?" He was anxious to please her; to pick up the contact they had lost what seemed like ages ago. Supper was over by now in the camp and the kitchen crew was finishing their cleanup chores. But food was found and distributed. Ken joined them in the small dining area sipping on his mug of coffee.

"We still can't accommodate everyone to eat here," he chatted as his guests gobbled up whatever they had on their plates. "Most people take the food to their rooms; that saves us from washing dishes," he smiled sheepishly.

The long barracks, eight in all, paralleled each other in the large courtyard of the camp. A corridor sliced each building in the middle, which led to the bath facilities at the end. Rooms opened into this hallway, with six to ten beds in each. The camp was not segregated in any way. Families lived together with singles, each person occupying a single cot. The arrangement was good to allow friends and relatives, if there were any to stay together. A table occupied the middle of each room for eating, playing cards, and writing letters home. Personal belongings had to be stored in cardboard boxes under the beds. In some rooms bunk beds were provided, mainly for married couples, where the upper unit served for storage and an extra blanket hung from it to give some privacy.

Erika was given a cot in a smaller room. An old couple and a middle aged single man stayed in there, the rest of the residents were single girls, who had all escaped from a college dormitory and knew each other. Imre found his place only two doors down the hall.

Wynn was ready to take his last trip back to the old camp. He called Ken to his office for final instructions. He lifted an envelope from his desk. The word "Confidential" seemed odd. It came from the International Red Cross Headquarters in Switzerland. He glanced through the brief message and waited for Ken to sit down.

"That girl, the one who just came in, how old is she?"

"I'm not sure," Ken was contemplating, "She says 18, but I think she's more like fifteen or sixteen. Why?"

The boss shoved the confidential letter across the table to his assistant. It was an official reminder to all camp commandants of the international agreement made at the end of World War II whereby, all children under the age of sixteen without a supervising family member had to be returned to their homeland by April 1, 1957. No conflicts of any kind, war or revolution, were exempt from this agreement.

"Well we must do something about this," Wynn said quietly as he stood up. " Try to find out her age, her family, perhaps both." He grabbed his briefcase and walked out of the office. The little green Bug sputtered away.

Ken knew very well that Erika was under the age limit; he also remembered that she had no living relative on this continent. He also knew that her father was somewhere in the U.S. There must be thousands of Molnars, a very common family name in Hungary, to search through. He must have more information on this; he must speak to her.

How do you approach such a sensitive subject? How do you ask a girl about her age without telling her why, without telling her that she is in grave danger? No, in the meantime he had to concentrate on the father. Lying about her age could come later, if everything else failed.

"How many Molnars are in the United States?" he finally asked her. It was a day or two later, but he maneuvered the conversation to it and waited.

"Why?" She looked at him suspiciously.

"We must find your father."

She was sitting on her cot; Ken was leaning against the wall. They were alone. She dreaded this moment, and no matter how many times she had tried to rehearse it, she had no clue what to say.

'Why?' There is always a small escape route from a dilemma by asking a small question like 'why?' Like when little girls are apprehended in mischief, when they are told that it is wrong, it's easy enough to just ask 'why?' Sure, we know why, but it gives us some time to delay the consequences.

"My father not Molnar," she blurted out suddenly.

"Oh, I did not know. Is he your step-father?"

She wasn't sure of the meaning, but it sounded like an acceptable term. It must mean good. It was also her salvation.

"Emanuel Klein his name. He can be anywhere."

Ken felt better, but not relieved yet. The name sounded German if not Jewish. He must try the latter first. Her age never came up. Imre walked in to save him from further agony in this investigation. Ken quickly excused himself and left.

"You won't believe the idea this guy came up with," Imre said when they were alone again. He led her to the window and pointed to the mountain across town. "See that plateau up there? He wants to build a huge cross and erect it up there to commemorate our great fortune to be away from communism. He wants to bring back Jesus Christ into our lives. He also wants me to help drag the cross there. Since I'm big and all." Imre was staring up the mountain, probably visualizing how the project could be done, or even envisioning the cross up there already.

Timber for the cross was easy enough to find. Millions of pines covered the mountains of Tirol; two large pieces were no problem. A small procession followed the huge object carried by dozens of strong arms. A local priest led the group through the narrow streets to the edge of town where the road serpentines toward their plateau. The rest of the camp waited patiently in the courtyard. When the cross was finally erected, the crowd cheered and applauded, while busy hands covered the base with heavy rocks to form its foundation. The priest offered a silent prayer.

There were many crosses in the mountains of Tirol,

strategically located at intersections of tiny roads and trails; not large or elaborate ones, just a simple crucifix, a rooftop shaped board protecting it from the elements, but almost always decorated with stems of flowers and colorful ribbons. These were the places where mountain folks gathered on Sunday mornings for a makeshift service, where they stopped occasionally to give thanks for a good day of harvest or for the birth of a healthy child. Tiny churches also dotted the countryside, big enough only for four or six people to kneel down, and without anyone knowing their denominations.

By the end of January, the whole camp had heard about the age limitation and waited quietly for the imminent roundup of their adolescents. Erika was aware of it also; she learned about it on the first day she took her volunteer job at the camp's mailroom. Correspondence between family members on both sides of the Iron Curtain had evolved quickly. The term 'Iron Curtain' was new to most of the refugees, but it was uplifting to learn that their struggle and sacrifice was made against such a strong, even if invisible, opponent.

The camp, besides food and lodging, provided each person with five cigarettes a day and ten shillings of Austrian currency a month. Most of that went for postage stamps. While sorting the incoming mail and inserting it in alphabetical cubicles on the dining room wall, Erika realized that her days of freedom were numbered.

16

Gefahr Pass, just above the village of Pertisal, connects Achensee to the main artery of Tirol, the Inn River. The mountain road, with treacherous curves and bends is well known to local drivers, but when a sudden snow squall blinds motorists and the slippery pavement provides no grip at all, anyone can face catastrophe. When the little green Volkswagen bug was found at the bottom of a ravine, authorities called the nearest Red Cross.

Andrasy took the message and ran to look for Ken. He was so upset he could not get out of the language lock his mind was in. Babbling uncontrollably in Hungarian did not help much. It took a few tries to convey the sad information that their beloved Commandant was dead.

Ken immediately called Vienna. It was decided on the spot, that Ken Williams, if only temporarily, was in full charge of Lager-A. With a staff of four and 613 residents, he could not believe the gravity of his situation no matter how many volunteers were at his disposal. "Can I get some help here," he begged his superiors, "I'm the only Red Cross worker now. I don't know how Wynn managed it, but I'm too new at this. I'm too new to this..." He did not realize he was mumbling; he sat in Wynn's chair, still feeling his warmth, trying to grasp the unbelievable.

'*Williams*,' his nametag declared in small white letters on a light blue plastic shield. Just that. No mention of Commandant or anything. Just Williams, who now must provide welfare, support and safety for Lager-A, the sprawling refuge in eight long barracks. He thought of his 24 years on this earth, his struggles with childhood, boyhood and the manhood he was so suddenly forced into. Working for the Red Cross, even if it was his own choice and decision, even if it was to benefit mankind, was now an awesome responsibility.

He remembered his after-school trip to Union Lake with his third grade buddies. They walked out on the pier for small boats and looked down at the water five feet below. And John Wharton, who was at least six inches taller than any of them, suggesting they swim out to that small island, and Ken admitting that he could not swim, and how John Wharton suddenly shoved him. "Now you do," he screamed and everyone laughed. Ken came up for air and sank again. Then human instincts took over; he began to dog-paddle from the bottom of the lake, pushing earnestly to save his life. John Wharton was never a good pal of his after this, but Ken did manage to become friendly to water. Today, he felt he was shoved into unknown waters again, and he must remember how to dog-paddle.

Registering refugees was a routine process; indoctrinating newcomers, issuing their personal supplies and clothing, keeping the kitchen turning out three meals a day for everyone; it all piled up on his desk now. Ken wandered through the main building first, checking all the functions, procedures and activities which no one had ever been trained for. He walked the endless corridors of the barracks, checked for cleanliness and listened to the cheery mood his constituency seemed to enjoy. His inner radar led him to

Erika's room. A small table radio was set at BBC and a few of
the girls were listening intently.

"British is dog barking," Erika said smirking. "I only
like American English, even if I do not know it yet."

"You are too young to be so particular," Ken
commented, but agreed that the accent was new to him also.
He tried to explain to them that he was the new
Commandant and why. He told them to be patient with
Great Britain because, who knows, someday they might wind
up there themselves. The age issue never came up at this time
either. He sat on Erika's cot for a few more minutes, then
walked out.

A commotion at the front of the dinning hall caught
his attention and he sped up to it. An ambulance had just
pulled in and its attendants ran into the kitchen with their
stretcher. The patient, he was told, was a young woman who
tried to lift a 400-pound cooking kettle to induce abortion.
She apparently lived with a man in camp when her real
husband showed up. She could not face him with someone
else's child. When she passed out, the ambulance was called.
Ken went to his office to make out a report.

"Find father?" Erika asked him from the open office
door a few days later. Things seemed to run smoothly for
now; a group of refugees were transported somewhere almost
every day. Camp Roeder in Salzburg processed several
hundred people daily who were headed for the United States,
but the 50,000 quota increase President Eisenhower pushed
through Congress gave them months of work. It was close to
the end of the workday and Ken enjoyed her visit.

"Yes, we have lots of fathers for you. So far, I
discovered seven Emanuel Kleins in the United States, not
one originating from Hungary." The search went through
several channels, including known Hungarian Clubs in the

States, but none came up. Erika had learned to understand 'none' very well by now. The days were zooming by toward the dreaded deadline, and Ken struggled through sleepless nights to come up with a workable solution. He called his Mother; perhaps she would sponsor Erika. On what, she wanted to know. Her almost part time clerking? It would not satisfy the Immigration Service. America needs an educated, experienced workforce, not a burden on its social service structure. New immigrants must be sponsored by an individual and be able to make a living by themselves.

By the end of February, while winter tried hard to hang on to its reputation, mild temperatures during the day helped making a snowman easier. Carefree living in the camp eased the pain of personal loss and the lack of language skills. Paul Toth made sure that behind the fences and between the walls of Lager-A everyone was safe. Safe from each other and safe from the outside world. His position as head of Camp Security posed a heavy burden on his shoulders and he took it seriously. Strangers living in close quarters sometimes got irritated at each other, the old felt lonely, the young restless.

Toth kept a suspicious eye on everyone. He had to, because he knew that an enemy could lurk from every cot in every room in every barracks. He knew how to recognize the ones who, just a few months ago, turned against the People's Republic of Hungary by becoming servants to reactionary capitalists of the western world. His job now was to collect and pass information on these traitors to his superiors in Budapest.

Toth was making his afternoon rounds. He was ready to spy on gatherings of insurgents of the failed uprising, continuously searching for lost comrades who escaped the conflict when the revolution seemed to be winning. The room seemed empty when he entered. He counted fourteen well-made beds, almost in military precision. Except the one in the left corner. The young man, snoring comfortably on the top of his blanket did not disturb the Security Chief, but the dirty boots on the blanket irritated him. He kicked at the boots with vigor. The young man opened his eyes and looked around in confusion. When he jumped towards the headboard he became wide-awake.

"You dirty bastard!" he screamed. "You are the one who beat me up at the AVO!"

"Get your fucking boots off the bed, you dirty slob," Toth replied with more surprise then anger. How could fate be so stupid, and at such a time? He swung around and left the room. He must report this to Andrasy immediately.

Hungarian leaders of the camp had their own small office now; separate from the Commandant; next to them was the camp's small mailroom. Volunteers took turns handling the hundreds of letters that came and went regularly. When Toth entered the office he took care to close the door to the post office too. He dropped down on his chair across from Andrasy, nervously tapping on the desk. With his other hand he grabbed the always-present toothpick in his mouth. He could never restrain his anger, not even when he was an officer of the AVO.

"We are in deep shit," he blurted out, taking out the toothpick. "There is a son of a bitch traitor out there who recognized me."

"Did you recognize him too?" Andrasy lifted his eyes from the Austrian newspaper he was busy with.

"Hell no! Some punk I supposedly reprimanded some time ago. But who keeps track of all that?"

"So, who is he?"

"Some country boy who was probably caught spitting on the sidewalk. But he is here now, and we must do something about him." Toth knew that Andrasy had better connections with not only the local authorities, but with Hungary also. He stayed in Austria after the war as a communist agent, part of the spy network that took over surveillance of that country after the Russian army pulled out. He got up and began to pace the room in deep thought.

"We must get rid of him immediately," he said finally.

"No shit," Toth remarked, "what took you so long to figure that out?"

"Don't mess with me," Andrasy spit back. "This is serious. If you get exposed, soon I will be too. So shut your filthy mouth and think."

"Is there a transport going out soon?"

"Good thinking. I think there is one early morning tomorrow." He searched his desktop for papers. "Yes, here it is. Twenty-four people at six. And guess what, they are heading to New Zealand. How far do you want to send him? Now, what's his name?"

"No idea," Toth mumbled, but he felt a bit more at ease. Somehow, he's going to get rid of the jerk. "All right. He is in room 27C, he was alone a few minutes ago, see if you can work on him. Bring him to your office and I will stop you if you have the wrong man." Andrasy had no problem getting the boy to sign up for a trip to the other side of the globe. A short call to Vienna fixed the deal, and their troubles were over. They did not imagine that on the other side of the mailroom door, Erika got an earful of the conspiracy.

She rose early the next morning not to miss the bus. The group was just about finishing their quick breakfast and had begun to line up for the departure. She ran up to the boy yelling, "You almost left without saying goodbye," as she threw her arms around the surprised kid. "Don't say a word, just listen," she whispered. "I overheard the two of them talking about you yesterday. Are you in some kind of trouble? Now, hug me and tell me what's going on."

"I'm going to New Zealand. Is that a problem?"

"Sure it is. They are getting rid of you in a hurry. Why?"

She grabbed onto the boy's free arm while he struggled with his luggage with the other. They passed Andrasy nonchalantly, heading towards the bus. "Give me your name at least."

"Horvath. Joska Horvath. Somebody painted anticommunist slogans on our dormitory walls... Toth wanted to beat it out of me. He is with the AVO, watch out." He stepped up on the bus, not looking back.

Erika turned towards the main entrance, bowed her head and began to cry. She passed Andrasy again and thought how easily she could get into acting. But this time she was also prodded by fear. Now she knew that Andrasy was in this, somehow.

"You are up early," Ken said coming out of the dining room. "We have that much mail?"

She glanced behind her as Andrasy was approaching them. Wiping her eyes she went straight to the mailroom. The mail had not arrived yet, she knew it, but if she stopped to talk to Ken, it would look suspicious. She waited within earshot as the two heads of the camp began their official business.

"Sorry to miss the bus," Ken said to Andrasy who followed him in. "I thought they would leave later."

"We had to expedite it somewhat. You know how these people in camp are, if they see a half empty bus, they all want to be on it."

"Any problems?"

"No! Not with me around."

Ken could not stand his Hungarian counterpart; his phlegmatic approach to everything, the know-it-all, self-assured personality. But Andrasy was a smooth talker, in Hungarian, of course, as well as German. Even, if you add his adequate smattering of the English language, he was still an important asset in the office. Except.. "Well, I must live with it," Ken was mumbling to himself. By this time Andrasy was in the mailroom. Sorting out the outgoing mail from the last day was a major chore; his help was well received even by the mailman himself. As soon as he walked in the room Erika spoke up.

"Never trust boys, never, never!" It was still part of the acting, a defensive move in case Andrasy would have any questions. He looked believing and went straight to work. Oh, the young, he thought, full of heartache. She piled the mail by countries now. Refugees were desperately looking for relatives all over the globe, anyone to sponsor them out of this camp. She made up tags for different bunches. With a folded paper in her hand she walked straight into Ken's office.

"I was upset before, sorry. I am rude with Boss." She handed the paper glancing behind her to see if Andrasy would follow. He was near their door, his head bowed, motionless. They knew he was listening.

"It is all right. I am sorry about your loss, but other boys will be coming around, just watch," gently folding out the paper in his hand while he talked. "MUST TALK, TAKE ME SOMEWHERE," the scribbled message said. He slowly folded it. "How about if we go to town for a nice espresso. I bet a little rum in it would cheer you up." He spoke louder than usual, insistence in his voice. Andrasy could not misunderstand the situation. It was quite early for such an excursion, but broken hearts cannot wait till the sun goes down. Or for any other convenient time.

She went back to the mailroom. "The Boss wants to cheer me up. How much more do we have to do?"

"Just go, get out of your mood. It will do you good," Andrasy said. A fatherly gesture, and a nice opportunity to make his private notes on where refugees were trying to go. He missed the opportunity last night tending to another problem at hand. He saw Toth in the dining area and waved him in. A long list of addresses and names had to be recorded, he could use the help.

A brisk walk to the nearest Coffee House was invigorating. They did not talk. Erika was formulating her report in her head; Ken could not imagine what this would be about. He suspected an incident that happened only a few days ago.

Erika was in his small quarters, the door ajar, working on her English lessons. Words were spoken, spelled out and written down, and organized in logical groups of topics to enhance comprehension. Objects around them came easy at first, then a pantomime of verbs with some struggle, a very difficult process of learning without the benefit of textbooks and dictionaries. But they seemed to have fun and she was pleased to attain and retain her lessons. He was pleased to be able to help, and to get a closer relationship. Even if she were not yet sixteen, Ken felt the almost eight years of age difference would be ideal. If only she could understand him a little better.

And how could he make her understand the word 'kiss,' for eventually he did bring it up. And the demonstration could not be made on the hand, the way gentlemen greeted ladies in European movies. No, that warrants more explanation, a deep cultural custom either party could not quite comprehend. A kiss had to be on the lips, not affectionate or sensuous, just a peck, just a little knock on the door to seek invitation. Of course the lesson ended quickly with light blushes on both sides. But Ken could not sense now if a passerby observing them started a rumor about this, or Erika's conscience awakened. He waited patiently.

Erika struggled with the taste of the rum. Even if Ken poured only a half a shot into her espresso, the flavor was there. "So, what's your problem?" he finally asked.

"Big, big problem," she said and went into a long explanation that needed her hands and arms. The spy ring that was connected to his camp, how Toth and Andrasy were passing on personal information to the communists back home, the witnessing boy's quick removal from camp, all that felt like big, big trouble to her.

At first, Ken could not believe such a possibility existed without his predecessor being aware of it, or not having acted upon it. He was a well-liked leader, or maybe he just used too much trust in his job. Maybe Erika misunderstood or misinterpreted the situation. But, if it were true that active spies surrounded him, what could or should he do about it? He represented only the helping hand of his country and was not a political overseer. What kinds of danger could his refugees be in from the information these people supplied to their superiors? Of course, it just dawned on him, the repercussion on their futures, no matter where they finally settled down; and the persecution of their family members left in Hungary.

Ken slowly planned out his responsibilities. He needed the immediate removal of the cohorts involved in this. But what proof did he have, and who were the others involved remained the big questions. Vienna must help in this. And there was Erika. Now there was physical danger looming over her also, so he had to do something, and do it fast.

17

"Mother, I made up my mind," Theresa said loudly. "I want to be the Chief Interpreter at the United Nations. I can speak Italian, German, and English already, now I am working on my Hungarian; it cannot be too difficult to learn the rest of the languages."

"You are only eleven years old," Mrs. Moscato giggled, "you don't have to work yet; I'll support you." She called two more helpers to prepare the meat for today's dinner. The refugee camp's large kitchen was full of activity, a never-ending preparation of meals. There were large kettles over wood fires, huge tables to work on, numerous sinks to clean vegetables and dishes. It was an enormous setup that cannot be compared to any other eatery in town, all under the knowledgeable supervision of Sophia Moscato, a World War II widow, who had separated from her family and country to become one of the thousands of Displaced Persons. For almost a dozen years, she and her young daughter lived in a small room in the barracks reserved for DPs next to the new Hungarian refugee camp. She worked in different places in town before, raising her only child, who turned out to be a genius.

No one could understand or explain Theresa's phenomenal sense for the art of languages. She began to talk long before she could crawl. Her working mother left her home in the care of different individuals in their camp, who spoke different languages. In the beginning she used both Italian and German as her native tongue. A Serbian woman stayed in the neighborhood for a few weeks, and Theresa picked up a few words quickly and learned new ones from other newcomers. By the time 1956 rolled around, the eleven year old war-baby knew some words from many languages and was well advanced in others.

English came to her for the first time in December when the Hungarian refugee camp opened and the American Commandant needed to hire her mother. "Please speak to me very slowly," Theresa asked in German, but the 'thank you' was already in English. She was allowed to sit in on all the managerial meetings with grownups, listening intently to every word said. She did the same thing while the Russians were the occupiers, but dropped her interest almost completely after the Soviets left.

Hungarian was a chore at first. "They talk funny," she told her mother. "The accents are at a different place in the words, and if I goof up they just giggle, but knowingly. I guess they understand me better than I do them." Erika kept the child occupied in the mailroom whenever she was around. They mixed and matched words from all the languages they knew somewhat, sometimes not even knowing whose tongue they were using. The importance of the few years of age difference quickly disappeared; they spoke freely about the goings on in camp, about boys and about how they missed their fathers.

But whenever the topic turned to Ken, Erika clammed up and changed the subject. She was not quite sure where their relationship stood. Was she a girlfriend to this mature young man, the highest authority over the large camp?

Was she in love, or just infatuated with the father figure, the embodiment of western civilization she was so earnestly trying to adopt? These were things that Theresa could not understand, in any language.

Erika went to Theresa's small lodging a few times, on her free time and they became close friends, able to communicate on many channels of which no other human was capable. Erika had learned how the Italian soldier died protecting the nazis, and told her young friend how she had fought the communist Russians. Once their wars were compared, there was no difference at all. The huge bloody political turmoil, squeezed into a short decade, placed them on the same side of the scale of history. And yet, they stayed young girls as much as possible. They took trips to the mountains that surrounded the small Austrian town, just walking the lonely snowless trails that showed very little that it was still winter in Tirol. They washed the few pieces of clothing they had together in the galvanized washbasins, and giggled quietly whenever men walked in to go to the adjacent toilet.

Ken was aware of the girls' friendship. Perhaps it was a way out of his dilemma. Now if he could get Erika to move in with the Moscatos, and she would stay out of sight, it should work. Just until he got rid of the bad guys. Communications, or the lack of it, presented its ugly head again. He could not talk to the mother; he could not rattle Erika with dangerous news, it had to be the child.

When they returned from their morning trip to the Coffee House, Ken sent Erika to her room to wait for him there. When he entered the kitchen, the normal chaos of the preparation of lunch greeted him. Europeans normally had their main course at noontime, and it needed the most prep work. He approached the mother nonchalantly.

"Theresa?"

"*Theresa es ist gut,*" she said checking an oven.

"No, no. Where is Theresa?"

"Oh. Theresa home."

'Great,' Ken thought. Where is home? He had never ventured to the DP section of the camp before. Not that it was fenced off or forbidden, but the long barracks had many rooms, and he had no idea where to even begin. The long corridor had entrances on both ends of the building; he picked the nearest one. An elderly woman appeared from somewhere.

"Moscato?" Ken approached her. She pointed towards the other end and mumbled something in an unknown language; perhaps it was a room number. Ken walked slowly down the empty corridor. The hall lights were on constantly in the windowless walkway. He listened intently for noises. A small radio was on somewhere and the faint sound came closer as he walked. It was a speaking voice and he realized it seemed to be a BBC broadcast. Ken decided that it must be Theresa's place. Who else would listen to English in this building? He tapped gently on the door. When it slowly cracked open, the young girl's relieved smile greeted him.

"Mister Ken?" Theresa moved the door wide open, as an invitation.

"Thank you," he smiled back and walked in. It was a small room all right. Two single beds lined up on one wall, a small table and two chairs on the other. The lone window in between opened toward the refugee camp. In the corner, a large wooden cabinet probably held all the family's possessions. Theresa pulled out the chair closest to one of the beds for Ken then she plopped down. Ken gladly took her offer.

The lopsided conversation went on quite a while. He spoke slowly and used a lot of 'yes' and 'no' sentences. When a 'no' was followed with a question mark, Ken stated the line again. At last, Theresa lifted both her arms and opened her palms like a stop sign.

"Andrasy and Toth," she said lowering her voice, "spies. No?"

"Yes, they are. They want to force Erika to go back to Hungary," Ken said also whispering. "We must hide her."

Theresa shook her shoulders shivering and in deep thoughts. "Two skinny girls sleep here," she said finally stroking the pillow next to her.

"Just for a few days," Ken said almost apologetic. "I'll get you another pillow. She can't leave this room, you understand?"

"Theresa understand," and she smiled. "I get Erika, OK?"

"OK!" And he went back to his office relieved.

The door to the Commandant's office was always open and this time the guest chair in front of his desk was occupied. A young woman stood up as Ken walked in.

"Commandant Williams? I'm Julia Jason from Camp Roeder. They sent me to help you out." She did not have to explain much more, her American Red Cross uniform filling in the rest of the situation.

"That is great," Ken greeted her and extended his hand. He had picked up the European custom of shaking hands, even with American women. She followed suit.

They sat across each other, the large desk imposing between them. He grabbed two cups and filled them with coffee without asking. His mother had sent him a Westinghouse coffeemaker from home, and they indulged in a weak, but real American brew. She explained how she drove the smallest Fiat management could spare from Salzburg, the American processing camp.

"When did you get here?" he asked, surveying his new assistant. 'Not bad,' he thought, the slim figure, the short hair, the flow of homegrown English, all pleased him.

"Oh, a few minutes ago. I left Salzburg early before they could change their minds. It's a madhouse there; a constant movement of people, anxious and nervous, the sounds of a foreign language; this lull here is refreshing." She went on to relate how the refugees were processed, the political inquisitions since they surely didn't want any communist to slip into the US, the medical tests since they surely didn't want any bad disease slipping into the country either. And yet, all these people have to be fed and housed. She told him about the large, makeshift bedrooms with people of all ages piled in, the self-appointed leaders picking up and distributing meals to them. "There were times when all we could do was to serve just canned Spam and dill pickles," she recalled, and told Ken how demand hugely surpassed supplies sometimes, and how patient the refugees were. "I feel these people will make good, progressive citizens for us, if we could only do more for them now."

Finding lodging for Julia posed yet another problem. Erika had been moved recently to a small, four-bed room with all single girls; perhaps Julia wouldn't mind taking her place.

"I'm sure it will be fine," she said. "I left a room like that in Kansas not too long ago. On the farm, you share with your sisters; here I can feel the same, even if I can't understand what they are saying. Less arguments this way."

Ken asked Andrasy to come in and made the introductions. He didn't want to mention Erika's absence, but he had to.

"I think she moved in with some new friends," he bluffed.

"Wouldn't it be up to me to approve such a change?" Andrasy complained. "If we don't keep track of things, there will be chaos here, would there not?"

"I'm sure everything is all right," Ken went on. The Hungarian was not pleased with more Americans crowding his territory, but he acted like a gentlemen. He kissed her hand and promised complete cooperation. They took the short walk to Building C, he carrying her single piece of luggage. The Fiat became the official car for Red Cross personnel. Both of them.

Julia became an irreplaceable helper in the processing department. Her experience at the main camp was useful now, even if her German was sketchy and her Hungarian nonexistent. She quickly learned to fill out the identity cards and the small gray typewritten forms, all in German. The individuals gave all the information, but it was kept simple. The names and dates came verbally, then were scribbled on pieces of paper, but many of the refugees had no legal papers to confirm them and no one asked for validation. Julia often thought how easy it could be to change some of that data for these people, and she wondered how often it was done.

Life became smooth and uneventful. She was pleased with that at first. But evenings were lonely and boring, Ken always being occupied or preoccupied with something. He skipped out of his office many times a day, and was almost never home in the evenings. It did not interfere with running the camp, but it sure annoyed Julia. She had to approach Andrasy somehow.

Her desk was placed next to Ken's in an L-shape to leave room for the visitor's chair. She had not wanted to move in with the Hungarians so she picked the cramped location. She asked Andrasy to join her while Ken was away. He graciously obliged.

"Would Madam care for some refreshment?" he inquired as he walked in. He always called her Madam which irritated her greatly, but it was too cumbersome to explain to him what the word meant back home. Slowly walking towards her desk he had both arms behind his back. When he got closer, he produced a small, green bottle and placed it in front of her.

"Nice apple wine from Burgenland," he explained while he uncorked the bottle. "My friends sending it to me, it's home made, very good." Without approval, he also pulled out two glasses from his pocket and filled them. "To our official cooperation and friendship." She clinked, barely touching his glass, for there was nothing else she could do.

"You've known our Commandant for some time," she edged into her topic, "was he always this busy, always out somewhere?"

"Well," he smiled and took the guest chair. "It is peculiar, is it not? A Commandant should be at his post to command properly." He took a sip of wine as he continued. "But he is a young man, and a man to be sure. I think he is out there to fill his manly needs. Is that not possible?"

She blushed lightly for a second. Exactly what was on her mind also. But it was just speculation on their part, was it not? She blushed again, this time for imitating the Hungarian in her mind. The truth had to be told, and she took a sip of the yellow liquid; what else could he be doing?

"We are operating this camp quite successfully with or without him, you and I, aren't we?" He smiled at his own approval. "But since we are dealing here with our problems, let me bring up something that's been bothering me for some time." He filled the glasses again; Julia seemed not to mind it.

"We have had a few disappearances here lately. Just before your arrival we seem to have lost a young man and a young girl. Not all together, mind you, but we haven't seen either one for a while, and we cannot find official dispensations of either one."

Julia was puzzled. People moved about, sometimes within the compounds of the camp; there were quite a few places where members found relatives or new friends and just changed bed spaces with others. And even if they had left camp, once they were processed they could wander out to find another camp; Austria had over sixty of them by now. She tried to explain all this to Andrasy. They broke up their meeting abruptly when Ken showed up.

"Don't stop now on my account," he said taking his seat. "What are we celebrating?" He glanced at the half empty bottle and the two glasses. "Sorry I missed it. I had some official business in town. I'll fill you in later." He began to read the dossier he had come in with. His two associates gulped down their drinks and were ready to disappear.

"Julia. May I have a word with you please?" It was more of a command. She looked as Andrasy inched out of the room with his party paraphernalia and sat back on her chair. Ken got up and closed the office door.

"We have serious problems here," he began. "I just came from the police."

18

"You look very cute when you're serious," Julia said when the Commandant looked up from his papers. "I guess I know why you were at the police station. The husband surprised you two, you got into a fistfight, and she called the cops. Naughty, naughty boy, you are." She smiled understandingly, inching closer with her chair.

"Nothing of the kind, I assure you." He showed embarrassment.

"Come on Kenny, we've been working together for days now and you haven't made a pass at me. Don't you think I'm good looking? Are you working too much to have a little fun?"

"We cannot discuss this now," he said abruptly.

"And why not? You are a nice young man with physical needs, you gallivant constantly, what else you are up to?" She laid her arms across the desk, almost trying to reach him, or just balancing her torso. The wine began to show its effects; she hid it behind an uncertain smile.

"Are you drunk, Julia?" He looked at her, searching for the signs. She lifted her palms to support her chin, her smile turned into a grin. Ken did not think this would work. "Are you able to discuss our problem, or should we pass on this until you are rested up?"

"Rest my ass, Your Honor!" She giggled and covered her mouth. She must be drunk, she thought, normally she was not this free with her words. Her upbringing on a farm in the Midwest also came with deep Christian morals. She knew she must stop herself. Without a word she ran out of the office.

Sensing problems, Andrasy stood up as the Red Cross worker sped by. He glanced at the other American in the distance who sank back to his papers. Ken looked up and waved to him. "While you are standing, will you join me?" It was more official sounding than he really meant it. But he wanted to see how Julia's cohort would react, for he was sure something was going on behind his back. He hadn't seen Toth since the kid was evicted in a hurry. Now this partying on the job while he was involved with the local police all added up to no good.

But Andrasy held his liquor quite well. Perhaps his age and long usage kept his tolerance high. He walked into the room without a slur or stagger and he also turned official. "Yes Sir. What can I do for you?"

'You can kiss my ass, you dirty bastard,' Ken wanted to say, but "Mister Andrasy, have you seen Erika lately?" came out. He needed to know what the other guys knew, to see if his efforts were successful in hiding the girl.

"No Sir. As a matter of fact, I have not observed her or talked with her for a few days now. Can you check our records to see if she already left the camp?"

"Now that is quite possible, you know." Ken started to relax. "In that case, never mind. When Julia comes back, she can look it up. How about Toth?" Ken ventured a bit further, "He seems to be out a lot also."

It was Andrasy's turn to get a bit pale. No one questioned Toth's whereabouts, not management anyway.

He knew very well where the guy was; he was back in Vienna right now, delivering the goods to the Soviets. "I am terribly sorry, sir, but I neglected to report to you that," his mind desperately racing for some acceptable excuse. "Yes," he almost smiled inside, "He has learned that his elderly mother crossed the border and he went to escort her here. I hope it doesn't inconvenience you in any way. The security brigade is working fine, at least there are no problems at present."

Ken was thinking. If the security people did not find Erika yet, it might just be safe for her. But what kind of security does the camp have? Perhaps it is for the better to have amateurs taking care of it. He would get Erika out of here soon, no matter what. He needed only a few more days. The police were on his back also.

Ken had been called by the police for a private meeting with the help of a capable interpreter who was also a policeman. Word had come down from Vienna that certain elements of the communist underground network were saturating some of the refugee camps; collecting and transferring information back to Hungary. An eyewitness had told authorities that a man named Paul Toth was present at Lager-A. Toth had crossed over to Austria in the first few days of the revolt when the Russians had not blocked the border. Austria received him with open arms, one of the first heroes bringing reliable news to the West. He worked his way down to Ebsen without gathering suspicion.

Now, Austrian authorities wanted to break up the spy ring, finding Toth first. Ken Williams could not imagine how quickly the communists set up operations, how despicably they had brought their fight with the revolutionaries into Austria. The pressure of his position began to affect him. He felt he had matured ten years in the last few days. What had he gotten himself into? Does helping others, doing good for mankind come with so many headaches? He wished he were back in a flood or an earthquake disaster somewhere, where he could fight the elements and not have to contend with seemingly normal people. But who is normal? Or what? He was told that communism is an ugly thing, a wart on the face of the earth, a disease that must be eradicated before the whole world dies. And does the flood of innocent people running away from it not prove this true? Will the help of God stop the atrocity and cure humanity? Will prayer help?

Ken Williams knew that there was no time for prayer now. April first was just around the corner; he must obey international laws and turn Erika over to her people. He also knew that Paul Toth and all his gang would stop him from rescuing her. He must find her father. First he must ask Andrasy to report to the police about Toth, then he needed to make another call to Vienna. There must be a man named Klein in America who would admit to being related to this pretty girl. And he needed to find out fast.

Lunch was over by now; Ken did not have the stomach to eat anything. He searched for Mrs. Moscato. She was on a well-deserved break before the preparations for supper would begin. Ken walked out of his office and headed in the opposite direction of Erika's hiding place. He went through the first barracks, looking attentively around as if he were on duty. He passed through the corridor and exited at the other end. Then he made his way towards the DP section. There was no one near the back of the buildings to observe him.

All the girls were in the room. Erika eagerly ate the lunch brought to her. Sophia Moscato rested on her cot, her eyes closed. When Ken knocked she did not move.

"Just checking," Ken said smiling. "How are you doing?"

"How do you do, too," Erika smiled back. "The prisoner is doing fine. You bring good news?"

"Almost good. Toth is back at the border and Andrasy is busy in his office. We could sneak out to get you some fresh air. After you are finished of course."

But she was finished, even if most of her food was still on her plate. Getting out of the room, no matter how welcomed she was there, uplifted her spirits. She stopped at the front of the small mirror hanging over the washbasin and gave a few strokes to her hair. "I am ready," she said throwing a cardigan over her shoulders.

It was almost springtime weather outside. They walked slowly, comfortably, admiring the sparkling snow on the surrounding mountainsides. The small brook outside the camp's fence pattered brief messages from the mountain peak to the young pines lining its banks. She held on to his hand, familiarly, transferring his body heat to warm her attitude to her predicament. She felt good being with him. She hoped there would be a solution.

Andrasy was leaning on the railing of the office porch. He too, enjoyed the last rays of the winter sun, puffing away eagerly, taking in the view. His hand in mid air held the cigarette butt he was ready to throw away. "Shit, it is her!" he mumbled taking a last drag. He retreated to the office almost too quickly. They did not see him.

'Where did she come from?' Andrasy wondered. He did not dare get into Ken's office to search for the exit log of the refugees. He badly needed Julia. "Where the hell is she now," he said loudly. He had to find her.

Three refugees and Julia lived in the small room. Their communications were restricted to giggles and hand signals. The girls did not mind the American, perhaps it was even beneficial to their everyday needs. They would get faster service, more clothing and shorten their food line. When Andrasy entered, without knocking of course, Julia was spread out on her cot, sleeping off the wine. He gently shook the toes of her shoes.

At first she did not know where she was, and then she wondered why the Hungarian chief was in her room. "It's me, don't be frightened," he said quietly, not to be overheard through the thin walls. "We must talk."

"Go ahead and talk," she said coming more to life.

"Not here, we must go to your office."

They walked quickly, he, almost dragging her, she, glancing around to see who would take notice. But life in the camp was buzzing as normal. People passed them without acknowledgement. No one liked the Hungarian boss much and no one could talk to the Red Cross worker. When they entered the front porch, Andrasy searched for his Hungarian counterpart. There was no one in the room.

"Get me the records on who left the camp in the past few days. Look for Erika Klein." The office doors were open as usual; he let her approach the desk, he stayed back on its other side.

"What the heck?" she said glancing at the piles of papers strewn around. The 'Klein' dossier was on the top. She grabbed the whole bunch and brought it to him as they walked to his desk. There were at least half a dozen request forms to the Red Cross, asking for the whereabouts of one Emanuel Klein.

"If he is looking for this guy now, the girl must still be here. Why did he say that she probably left?" He quickly explained to Julia why Erika had to be transported back to Hungary. "If my boss is up to no good," Julia said almost to herself, "I have an ace up my sleeve, don't I?" Andrasy did not get the connection. But Ken did. He was standing in the doorway with both arms blocking the opening. "I didn't know you guys were gamblers," he said smiling. As he finally turned toward his office, Julia stepped front of him before he could see the Klein files. "I was just looking for you." She was thinking fast now how to get her boss out of the office. "I found Erika Klein for you," she finally said.

Ken slowly turned to face her, hoping that she was only a mirage.

"Yes, she was in our room just now, looking for something she probably left behind there," she explained to the baffled Commandant.

"It is not possible," he blurted out. "I mean, how is that possible?" Is the game over, he wondered, or were these two playing a different game? "Are you sure?"

"Sure I am sure. She was there only a minute ago. You want to see?"

Ken got more confused now. He quickly assessed the events of the past hour or so. He thought about their cozy chitchat at the fence, their admiring remarks on the beauty surrounding them. Then the slow stroll back to her barracks, holding her hands and squeezing them before she walked into the DP building. Then came the realization that his duties were calling, he had serious problems to solve. He was sure he had made the short walk to the office quite quickly. How could she go to her old room without him observing it? What was going on here? But he could not ignore Julia's invitation.

"Ok, let's all see this," and motioned to Andrasy to come along.

"Just one minute, please, and I be with you. Nature calls." It was true; he did have important things to do. The dossier had to be returned. He was walking out of the office a few minutes later as the Americans were coming back. "She is not there," Julia informed him.

"So, where can she be?" Julia chided, like it was somebody's fault.

"She is on her way to Salzburg," Ken finally admitted, "I sent her there."

"Is this documented?" Andrasy wanted to know.

"It's on my schedule. She just left," Ken said when the phone rang. Andrasy picked it up, the only one in the room capable of handling German. After a short conversation he hung up.

"Why are the Austrian Police looking for Toth?" he confronted his Commandant.

"That's what we were supposed to discuss earlier," Ken raised his voice. "Can someone explain to me how a former AVO officer can work as Security Chief in this refugee camp? What kind of security procedure are we following here?"

Julia seemed to detach herself from these proceedings. She wanted to let the two guys fight it out. The Hungarian went on the defensive. "Like it is my fault now. People are moved in and out of this camp without my prior notification, they change rooms and there are no recordings of them. Well hell, I wasn't told about getting a new Red Cross person here either, or that the camp now has an official motor vehicle. I am…"

"All right, all right," Ken cut him short. "Perhaps that is all true. But isn't it also true that we have no written manual on running a refugee camp? We all try to do our best to get these poor creatures well and comfortable until we can pass them on to a better future. So let's work out the small details among ourselves without hard feelings." He sat at his desk now, picking up the nearest paper in front of him. The other two were stunned for a second and waited for what was coming.

Ken reached into the 'Klein' dossier and pulled out the documents. It was obvious to him that they had been tampered with. He was always neat, facing all the sheets in the same direction. "Now take this for instance," straightening out the pile while arranging his response. "This poor girl is desperately trying to find her father. I made seven tries, seven inquiries before my superiors finally succeeded." Perjury and its consequences rushed through his mind. 'The die is cast,' he admitted to himself, 'there is no way back.' "She is gone now, I hope she finds happiness. Now let's clean up this Toth affair. Any suggestions?"

Julia knew that her boss was lying about the girl. Was he risking his position for a young thing like that? How far was he involved with her? Was it worth it to her to chase after him and lose everything, or should she put her faith in the Hungarian? He was mature and intelligent, even into some money, too. She scrutinized his face, the smooth skin and tiny mustache, the receding hairline, a distinguished gentleman. Together, they could flip the Yankee kid out of here. Something to think about.

Andrasy, on the other hand, felt the Americans were crowding him. Was the little Jewish girl the trap they forged for him? The picture of them standing at the fence was still in front of his eyes. Did they know more about his operation? He was anxious to find out. "If our Security Chief is a spy, perhaps he is not alone in this?" He posed the question to his opponents to see where it would fall.

"He's got a few people working with him, perhaps some of them are also spies," Julia guessed honestly.

"Can you check this out?" Ken was seeing a way out.

"Not a bad idea," Andrasy relaxed a bit. "Can Julia back me up on this; people are more receptive to uniforms."

"Do you have the list?" Ken conveyed his approval.

Julia and Andrasy left and they found three young men to question. When they returned from their hunt, the Commandant's office was empty and the Fiat was gone.

19

Ken watched as his subordinates left his office. He knew their task was cumbersome and sensitive. They had to find and question some of the refugees to see if they were spies for the communists. Who would admit to such thing? And why were they so eager to do the search? Was Andrasy on the level? But, that was only one of the major problems Ken Williams was facing now. The other was Erika. She was cute, pleasant to be with, a fast learner and much too serious for her age, whatever her real age was. But who was hiding behind her pretty face? Time was getting short to find out.

His half-baked plan was not that complicated. He would take her from her hiding place, take Theresa with them and see who jumped to conclusions, who would throw the blame on him. He knew he must act quickly, must make the move now. The Fiat was always parked at the front of his office.

"Girls, we are going for a ride," he announced as he walked into the DP camp. Their giggling stopped. When those two were together, the world slipped back a few years to let them become kids again; to lie on the top of their cot resting their chins in their palms, saying silly things about boys; how funny their adolescent faces looked when the first dark shadow appeared under their noses. But a trip, that sounded exciting.

"Where to?" Erika wanted to know first. "Me too?" was Theresa's concern.

"We are going far away and together," Ken reassured them. "Get your little suitcase and take some of her belongings too," pointing to the younger one. "In the meantime, Theresa, you will write a note for your mother, and we are leaving in two minutes." He did talk calmly, like it was to be entertaining. But inside, he was a nervous wreck. He had everything on the line now, his integrity, his position in life, all for a selfish cause, to save Erika for himself.

Theresa fit nicely in the tiny back seat of the Fiat. Their luggage lay next to her. Ken searched the refugee area before turning the car into the main street unobserved. He checked the fuel gage and headed for Route 47 to follow the Inn River north. He knew what he wanted to accomplish, but had not verbalized it yet. He had a whole afternoon to work out the details. Fortunately, the girls did not ask again where they were going; he wouldn't know what to tell them. Some time later the road sign said 'Kufstein' and somehow, he wanted to go there.

The ancient little town was composed of rocks, stucco and timber. A bubbling river paralleled the main thoroughfare and earnestly tried to take all the moisture out of these parts of the Alps to dump it into the Inn. At the most appropriate location, people of hundreds of years ago built an impressive fort. High up on a plateau, pieces of stones were layered to form a bastion against intruders, attackers, and nomad scavengers. Different peoples occupied the fort from time to time; sieges were deterred or lost; only the stones survived for sure. By the middle of the nineteenth century the stronghold was made into a fortified prison for the enemies of the Hapsburgs, housing numerous infamous criminals and political opponents. Today, Kufstein, with all of its long colorful history, had become a well-liked tourist attraction. Ken wanted to spend some time there.

He parked the car right on the curb, a common practice on the narrow streets. Happy for free movement after being cramped in the little car, the girls felt great. Strolling by the tiny stores and restaurants, they turned into a long, uphill driveway protected by strong, high stone walls. The courtyard was a typical rectangular space where all the halls and rooms opened in ancient times. In the middle, a well still contained some water; at the far end, several hanging trees gave a gruesome reminder that the place was once a prison.

They walked the narrow tops of the walls, envisioning the hoards of enemies climbing on long ladders from the deep valley below. The cast-iron, rusty cannons, once emitting death and destruction, now lay quietly in front of their peepholes. Ken remembered the few such places he had visited on school trips, like Fort Ticonderoga on Lake Champlain in Upstate New York. He could not remember if that fort was really that much larger than this, or was it just that we see things as bigger when we are a small child. Death and Destruction. Why is it that mankind always has to use aggression to settle its differences? Ken wondered if there was a Red Cross at the times of these battles? Wouldn't it be better not to need either one? Climbing down on an old ladder to the courtyard brought him back to his own century. Obviously, the girls forgot it all as they were running up to the well looking for demons at the bottom of its deep shaft.

"Anybody hungry?" Ken said, catching up with them. There was no opposition to the idea. Not to get into problems with the selection of the eatery, they walked into the first one. Their table had three chairs and its fourth side faced the wide window overlooking the now busy street. Theresa took charge of ordering, unashamed to pick the best of the offerings. Erika stayed away from Coca Cola this time but Ken ordered the smallest glass of beer. The place was cozy and pleasant; their conversation concentrated on English, rugged at first, then smoother as their topics reflected more serious matters. They talked like three adults now. In turn, they brought back all their recent struggles from three different corners of the world.

Theresa had the shortest story to tell. She had been born and lived all her life in their little room. Trips to Innsbruck once or twice were the highlights of her life. "You know there is a house there on the main plaza that has a gold roof over the veranda?" She explained that a long time ago it was owned by a noble person or something, who became embarrassingly poor. To ward off ugly gossip, he turned all the family jewelry into gold planks. The admiration towards the rich owner now was overwhelming. But he still lost out somehow, because the place was now a wedding chapel. "People from all over the world are eager to go there and get married."

"This lovely meal and elegant surroundings," Erika remarked, "makes me feel I am at a wedding."

"Basically, you are," Ken spoke quietly. He desperately hoped to recite the lines: 'Will Erika Klein take Ken Williams as her lawfully wedded husband?' and the rest, but his words were less romantic. "If we tell people at the camp that we just got married, they can't take you back to Hungary, can they?" They ate their Black Forest cake in complete silence.

"You know where the Black Forest is?" Theresa finally spoke. "Straight west from here, right were the

Danube River ends, or starts." She was well aware of Erika's predicament, her underage status and all, but they had also talked a lot about her feelings toward Ken. It was like a cold shower to hear that romance in their lives was shadowed by lifeless political maneuvering; that their hopes were beginning and ending at the Black Forest. At least, the Danube had a chance.

"Thank you for your concern," Erika slipped back to their serious subject, "But it will not solve our problems. Everybody knows that I am too young."

"Not anymore," Ken said with emphasis. Reaching into his uniform's pocket, he produced a small, folded, gray paper, the official ID card provided for the refugees by the Austrian government. Erika picked it up and opened it. Only her birth year had been changed. She was an adult!

"I do not deserve to cause trouble for you. Not a criminal like me."

"What are you taking about? You are a refugee, chased out of your country by your own government. A little slip of the pen will give us time. Time to find your father and get you to America." The soothing words could not calm her anymore. Her mouth twitched and her tears began to pour. "They're going to find me, no matter where I am."

"Is there more than what's on this paper?" Ken asked to have the Pandora's Box opened. How come they never spoke about her past in detail? How did he miss the seriousness of her sad moods? Why is this lovely child a woman in sorrow?

"Yes, more. A lot more. I was scared and angry. Very angry. Still, I didn't have to kill so many of them!" Lunchtime patrons of the house began to take notice, the waiter needed to know if there was a problem with their meal. Ken paid their bill and escorted the girls to the car. Theresa was interested in hearing how the things would come out that she already knew.

Erika did not know, or care, where they were driving. But she tried to compose herself and spoke quietly about the ugly past, about the dark, heavy burden on her soul that did not want to let any sunshine in. Sure, she had a few somewhat happy moments, even fun here and there, but she did see the destruction and carnage she had so quickly caused. The images of the burned bodies, the missing limbs, the lost lives shadowed her life every day.

"I don't understand," Ken said. "You did not start all that, you only hit back. You are our hero. Your name will be on a monument somewhere, someday. Besides, you are in a safe haven now. Nobody will harm you."

"They will if they can. They chased me at first, now they are searching for me."

"There is no such thing," Ken assured her.

"I have witnesses of the highest rank." It was time now to bring up Frank. Frank, her sweetheart whom she had lost, but also Frank's father, the fearless political leader the whole revolution was against. She also knew deep in her heart, that the AVO would do anything to take revenge on her.

Ken knew of the intense power of communist oppression, but this was the first time it hit his soul. The whole story was a shock. It was known through the media how young people, perhaps very young ones, took their places in an insurgency. But those were boys! Boys who learned to fight in kindergarten playgrounds. But Erika? His Erika? He tried to visualize the described event. To see the Devils in the gloomy night. And as more and more pictures came to mind, he found it more fascinating. She was a hero! She was a real freedom fighter. Then he thought of Toth and his cohorts in Lager-A. And if they were selling information, why would they not sell something more? As the little Fiat turned into the camp, Ken Williams determined that even if he had to chain Erika to himself, he would never lose sight of her.

20

Andrasy knew there was no need to interrogate the young men who eagerly signed up to be policemen for the camp. They came to serve; not only was it something to do, but there was also a certain amount of prestige, a rank they never experienced before, over the multitude of refugees. They were nice boys, happy to be useful, and they were cleverly kept out of their boss's little shenanigans. Only the missing commandant was the mystery.

As they walked into the office the phone rang, Andrasy grabbed the receiver. It was Toth. He was in Vienna waiting for the train to take him back to Tirol.

"Not so fast," Andrasy warned him. " That kid must have talked to someone and the local police are looking for you. We should have drowned him or something, do you hear me?"

"Yes, I hear you. You are full of good news. But I didn't call you for that. Forget about underage refugees, we have a bigger fish to catch. Where is the little Jewish girl?"

"Just that. We can't find her. Our Commandant is playing footsics with her. The son of a bitch is lying to us. Something screwy is going on here I tell you."

"No! Tell me where the little bitch is!"

"All right. What's the big rush?"

"I tell you. The word here is that the Soviets are willing to pay a good sum for her. Every agent is searching for her, and we should get the prize money. We have her."

"I don't get it. Why is she so important all of a sudden?"

"It's a long story, but basically this is what it's all about. Supposedly, she blew away a bunch of Russians in Budapest. Now she is called 'The Butcher of Duna Street.' And they want her, badly. So get her."

"It is easy for you to say," Andrasy shot back, "But while I am looking for the Jewish girl, our young American boss is gone too."

"So who is in charge?"

"I am, for Christ sake, and I'm the one who has to find the girl. And I'm the one who has to come up with a cockeyed story why we have to send a revolutionary hero back to Hungary? Are they going to give her a medal or something?"

"All that is their problem. Just find her!"

There was a bit of confusion on who was the boss over whom for a minute, but with the conversation all in Hungarian, at least the American was unaware of what was going on. "Call back every hour, on the hour, until this is taken care of. You got that?"

Toth hung up.

"We have to get some papers out of Mr. Williams' office," he finally turned to Julia. "Vienna wants us to send them the children. There is a bus waiting up there to take them to Hungary. Where the hell is Williams?"

There was no list to be found in the Commandant's office. Actually, Julia was not much interested in the whole matter. She just wanted to help Andrasy out, to get on his good side, and who knows, if Williams really screwed up badly, maybe there was a top position in the camp for Julia Jason.

"Maybe we'll just send up the Jewish girl," Julia made an effort to command.

"Sure! Go get her!" There was enough sarcasm in his voice for her to pull back.

From the other side of the corridor they heard the sobbing of Mrs. Moscato as she wobbled towards them. She was continuously wiping her eyes with the corner of her ever-present apron; in her other hand, she grasped a piece of paper that she was certain would explode at any minute.

"*Theresa, mein Theresa,*" she cried turning over the paper to Andrasy. It was a childish scrawl in Italian.

"What is it?" he inquired in German.

The simple note informed the heartbroken mother, that her only child had accompanied the American camp Commandant and his Jewish girlfriend and they were taking her toward the German border in their Fiat right now.

"The son of a bitch kidnapped this poor woman's daughter," he angrily translated to Julia. "And we don't have anyone to send to Vienna either. The threesome is probably going to Munich, the American Army Base." He dropped down on his chair to figure out what the problem was, or if there was a problem, and whose problem it really was. Then he thought of the price on Erika's head. He rubbed his eyes with both hands and tried to think straight. Now he remembered the early morning scene boarding the bus a few days ago. The sobbing girl saying farewell to the boy they smuggled out in a hurry, and the pretentious parade into the Commandant's office. A clear picture emerged in Andrasy's head. The girl must know about the AVO interrogation. She must have overheard their evacuation plan the night before, why else was she up at the bus so early? And the

Commandant too knows everything by now. He is the one who alerted the police. But he couldn't have told them everything. He doesn't even know the monster he's harboring. He must be stopped. There must be a way. Finally he turned to Julia.

"How much criminal immunity do Red Cross members have?" Mrs. Moscato was still under the spell of her loss, even more confused by the English words.

"A crime is a crime," she said in deep thought. "Kidnapping is very serious, if that's what you're mulling about."

"Yes. And two innocent young victims, and abandoning hundreds of poor suffering people under your charge, and crossing over to another country with the camp's stolen property. How long you want the list to be?"

"Herr Commandant!" The voice came from the open office door. The young man standing there blocked all the light in the doorway.

"Yes, son?" Andrasy blurted out, annoyed by the interruption. The rapid flow of Hungarian language bypassed all the others in the room. The inquirer had been searching for the Security Chief for days. He was reluctant at first to intrude on the Commandant, but time was running out, he explained; some people in his barracks were getting restless, and he would like very much to help out, if only he could be appointed to security duty.

So, that's all their problem? Just getting restless. How nice of this big boy to come to rescue our camp. "What's your name, son?"

"Imre, Imre Kish, at your service," he smiled politely.

"All right, Kish, you are appointed. Do you want a ceremony with it?"

"No sir, not at all. I only have one question. Am I authorized to arrest and hold anyone deemed dangerous to the peace and welfare of this camp?"

"Of course you are," Andrasy reassured him. "Who is big enough to stop you?"

He briefly explained to Julia what was happening, how things were going to shape up nicely, how this blob of a giant would help them straighten things out.

"Welcome aboard, my man," he said with all the seriousness he could muster. He walked up to him and patted, or at least he tried to reach his shoulders. "Now, Patrolman Kish, what will be your first official duty?" Andrasy winked towards the others, Mrs. Moscato was still totally confused.

"With all due respect, sir," the new security guard said sternly, "I am placing you under house arrest until more qualified authorities can take over here. Please go into the mailroom where you can be locked up."

"Are you a raving idiot?" Andrasy shouted. "Do you know who you are talking to?"

"Yes, sir, I do. I know exactly who you are. My father warned me about you before I crossed the border. You are Colonel Count Erno Andrasy, Assistant Chief of Intelligence of the Imperial Hungarian Army during World War II. Ex Chief, that is. You left the service of Admiral Horthy in 1943 when he resigned as Regent of our country. Presently, you are selling personal information about the people of this camp to the communists in Hungary. Am I correct, Count?"

Andrasy slowly backed away from his accuser and plopped down on his chair. Glancing around the room he suddenly realized that this horrid conversation was securely between them. The curious faces of the other two reflected intense curiosity but no comprehension.

"What a speech," he finally got his voice back. "Too bad no one understood what you were babbling about. You want me to explain to them how wrong you are?" He got up now to face the boy, leaning back against his heavy desk. "Some points you made are correct, of course," and he tried to smile. "But it was a war, you understand. I was on the wrong side of a war serving some awful people. But a soldier must follow his orders. I did it well. And when my Admiral resigned I followed him in that too." He slowly turned to the others. "We are having some recruiting problems here, ladies. It may take some time, so if we could be alone, we would appreciate it." He made the request in two languages, reassuring the camp's chef that he would look into her predicament also.

When they were alone, his anger flared up again. "You are a stupid jerk, you know! If you were a real soldier you would be court-martialed right now. I am a respected citizen of Austria. How do you think I got this job anyway? I was appointed by the government of this country. How dare you to come here, freeload on the generosity of this land and insult me. Sure, there was a request for the information you are talking about. Sure, I provided some. But what kind of information? Adulterated, for sure. How many people here do you know with their real name, or age, or marital status? Most of them are hiding something. They are desperately trying to alter their past to suit their present and modify their future. We fill out these documents on their say so." Andrasy hit a pile of papers on his desk with a clenched fist. "They all have some false information in them, and that's what I was selling to your countrymen." He cut the long speech and lowered his arms exhausted. "As a matter of fact, what are you hiding behind your ugly face? Are you really who you are telling me you are? What do you want to do? Hang on to your stupid assumptions of me, or go back to your barracks and tell your *compadres* to play some cards, or jerk off to soothe their restlessness. Let us run this place the best we can."

Imre was stunned by the verbal avalanche. The truth, his truth, was bouncing back and forth in the room like a live ping-pong ball. And at the end, who was he to throw the first stone? Wasn't he too hiding behind a face he could not change? What if Andrasy suspects something? Are there any more punches coming from the Commandant if he didn't retreat now? "I just want the girl back," he finally said quietly.

"What girl?"

"Erika."

"You see, you are doing it again. You are pissing me off. Don't you know that she is with the American? Right now, she is in his arms. Why did they take off from here, you think? She is gone, gone from you anyway."

The phone rang and Andrasy jumped to it. It was Toth, his hour was up. "Hold on," he said, "I have to get rid of an intruder." Imre did not wait for instructions.

"There is no news yet. Did they give you any money for the other work? I told you I want American dollars this time, did you get them? Oh, shit!" he shouted suddenly looking through the office window. "They are back! All three of them are back! Listen, whatever you do, don't come here. Meet me in my house in Kufstein tomorrow night. You think you can make it? And bring the dough!" He hung up without waiting for an answer and approached the entrance door. A smiling group of people walked in.

"Well, well," Williams said, "The house seems to be in order." He stepped aside to make room for the Italian family reunion. As Theresa and her mother cried happily, he got closer to the Hungarian Commandant. "Now, congratulate us and meet the new Mrs. Williams," taking the grinning Erika's hand to move closer.

"Are you crazy? She's only a child!"

"She turned eighteen last month."

Andrasy could not believe his ears. He was sure her papers showed no such thing. He had written them up himself. There must be a conspiracy going on here, but how could he prove it? "I don't believe you," he said just the same.

"Sorry to hear that, but our marriage papers should be here in a couple weeks. You see, we traveled to Munich to get this done on our base. A piece of cake. She is not only my lovely bride now, but she will accompany me to the U.S. of A. when I am not needed here anymore."

'You are not needed here right now,' Andrasy thought. But he wanted the girl. Married or otherwise. If possession was ninety percent of the law, he knew, he would succeed. Maybe he and Toth could figure out something tomorrow.

Ken escorted his new bride into his office and closed the door. He needed to work out a plan for keeping the bad guys away from her, how to catch the bad guys, and how life would flow after all these were worked out. For he was the only one who knew that there would be no marriage license coming. That for the time being, Erika was safe only with him. Sleeping in his office chair for a while would be a small price for that safety.

'You won't get away with this!' Andrasy thought angrily. 'I will make sure of that.'

21

Andrasy rented a small place in town for the duration of his assignment. It was a short walking distance from the refugee camp and it was used mainly for sleeping. He had his meals at camp and spent long hours in his office. Not that he was so conscientious about his job; but he did not want to miss anything that could be reported to the communists. It paid handsomely; the more pages, the more names, and the more detailed background information meant more cash in his monthly envelope. His permanent residence was in Kufstein, right on the main tourist drag. Even if it was right above his gift shop, the cozy apartment had all the comforts he needed in his close-to-retirement age, including a direct staircase to his work.

Tourists often stopped at the gift shop to pick and choose souvenirs from the hundreds of memorabilia reflecting the culture and history of the region. But customers came mostly to admire his handmade wall clocks, with the intricate designs and movements of colorful cuckoo timepieces that Andrasy artistically crafted himself. He did not sell a lot, but his pricey pieces brought in a nice income. In total, his shop was an amusing endeavor, a quiet, peaceful life after many years of turbulent times in war and politics.

When Toth walked into the store for the first time he looked and acted like any other tourist. He intently studied the shelves, the items hanging on crowded wall spaces, and bent down to the glass covered showcases, taking his time. Andrasy knew from experience that his customers were more receptive to his wares undisturbed. When they made they selections on their own, they were more willing to purchase. He stood behind his workbench and watched the lone visitor moving slowly between the isles. The tall, skinny, middle-aged man wore a long, drab raincoat, definitely not a well off foreigner. Finally, he was at the register with a couple of postcards, hardly requiring so much study.

"Count Andrasy?"

The words came in a perfect accent, which he hadn't heard in many years. "*Aufwarten!*" the owner bowed his head, subconsciously clicking his heels behind the counter.

"Then we should continue in Hungarian," the visitor said, "It is more comfortable." And they did. The subdued counter-revolution left a disorganized, badly damaged Hungary; a lot of unanswered questions, a lot of wrongdoers unpunished. But the revamped government feverishly tried to bring back law and order; its correctional institutions quickly filled with insurgents, the ones that could be caught. Others crossed the border to Austria. Lieutenant Toth had his assignment as part of the retribution. When he left the gift shop, the postcards remained on the counter, but a deal had been made. All Andrasy had to do was to arrange for the smooth running of his business in his absence, and to show up at Lager-A with the letter of introduction from the Austrian government. The camp badly needed, and greatly appreciated a distinguished gentleman with a military background to lead the hundreds of homeless refugees. Appointing Toth to be Security Chief closed the circle.

Today, Andrasy had to return to his home in Kufstein. He had an important visitor. He gave the young man who attended the store the rest of the day off and turned over the 'Closed' sign on the door, a visible signal to the small bar across the street. Toth was there in no time. They shook hands like old friends and made the slow ascent to the apartment above. Andrasy shut off all the lights in the store and pulled out a brandy bottle from the cupboard.

"You think we have something to drink to?" Toth smiled.

"Hope you came with some bright ideas and plenty of money."

"Not really, only some reports. The money will come as soon as we finish this assignment."

Andrasy wasn't pleased, but was willing to listen. They poured their drinks just the same and dug into the documents. Erika Molnar was the main subject. The report had all the details about the butcher shop; on Klein, its previous owner; the horrific attack on the Soviets near the front of the shop, and even a signed report by the building's superintendent. As the investigators searched through the details, they found it amusingly clever how Erika had been trying to cover her tracks with the name change to Klein.

"What happened with this Molnar guy?" Andrasy asked.

"Apparently he, too, was murdered in the attack, but his body was not found. Lots of burned people were scattered by the explosions."

"Are you sure he is dead?"

"I am almost sure."

"Perhaps he is not," Andrasy commented almost to himself. His dormant investigative brain seemed to get a jolt. Slowly a plan developed. The old man is alive but seriously injured. He is in a hospital in his last hours. He desperately wants to see his granddaughter. She must come to say her goodbyes. She must return to Hungary and in a hurry.

"Who is going to tell her?" Toth needed to know.

"We should have a letter or something. A note the gravely ill man dictated to a nurse, maybe. That's it. Here," he took a piece paper and a pencil. He shoved it to his companion. "You write it. Make it desperate and keep it simple. It's coming from an old butcher." The scribbling was short and to the point. They would tell Erika that a nameless refugee brought the folded, unsealed letter through the border. On the outside it was properly addressed to Erika Klein, just to make sure.

The following morning Andrasy called Erika in as she headed to the mailroom. When she took the seat across from his desk, he ceremoniously waved the letter in the air. "I have terrible news for you, I'm afraid," he began. "Your poor grandfather is very ill but wants to see you. I pray you'll be still on time."

"My grandfather?" Erika stood up in disbelief.

"Yes. It is here in writing. A nurse in the hospital wrote it down for him. Sounds like he was seriously injured in a battle of the revolution. He is hanging in there.. But why I am telling you? Please, read it yourself."

She unfolded the letter and could hardly read the childish lines. Her quiet tears clouded her eyes. It sounded impossible, but a flicker of hope twisted around in her mind. In such a short time, in the past few months, she had been led through a rugged terrain full of disappointments. Nothing seemed to be real anymore. Was it possible that her first step in the wrong direction may be reversed to be good? Is there a miracle for her after all? She sat quietly now, folding and unfolding the precious letter. Then, out of the foggy vision on her lap a mysterious reality emerged in two bold words: ERIKA KLEIN. How could Grandpa know that she was traveling under that name? She stood up, ready to leave. "I have arranged your transportation to Vienna already," Andrasy spoke up. "As a matter of fact, for your safety and comfort, I am the one who will escort you to the border. Our train leaves this afternoon."

"I need,... I have to... I must cry alone now," she finally mumbled as she ran out of the room. Outside of the building she was searching for the Fiat. It was parked at the back of the DP building. She walked at a deliberately slow pace, digesting her predicament. She saw her grandfather's body so helplessly stretched out on the pavement; she remembered Frank's description of the terrible scene. How was this letter possible? Yes, the old man knew perfectly well who Erika Klein was and who Erika Molnar was. Perhaps he wanted to make sure that the message would find her. And it did. What is wrong with this picture? Ken would know. Ken always knows.

She wiped her eyes and composed herself. She knew she must be strong and face whatever comes around the corner. They almost bumped into each other as Ken was coming out of the building.

"Here you are. I was looking for you everywhere."

"I am here now," she gave him a wry smile. They got into the Fiat for privacy, and she translated the letter for him. He took it for a minute and studied the lines, like it was hiding a code or something. Finally, he pointed at the signature. "What does this say?"

"It is his name: Molnar Geza, the Butcher." He always signed his letters like this, the very few he ever wrote. It is a distinction from, for example, "Molnar, the Tailor."

"I see," Ken mused for a while. "If this letter was meant for you, and only you, would you know this distinction by now? Wouldn't "Your Loving Grandfather" look better at the end of the page?" He opened the car's door and stepped out. Erika followed without being asked. "When is your train leaving?"

The question was a sudden letdown. He wants, he was going to allow her to return to Hungary, to an almost certain repercussion from her government. She would never see him again, not in this life. She walked toward her room to pack.

"Don't worry, it will turn out all right. I will think up something, I promise." A few minutes later they had their last lunch together. She did not notice what it was they ate. He sipped on a mug of black coffee. The minutes went by quietly, their goodbyes composed in their silence. When Andrasy walked in, the Commandant stood up and turned to him. "You win this time. Take good care of her." He walked away without another glance at his wife. It was peculiar, but it made Andrasy more comfortable. His assignment was working out nicely, and their train was coming.

22

They walked silently the short distance to the train station. Occasionally Erika glanced back towards the refugee camp, hoping, but there was no sign of Ken Williams anywhere. At least he could have offered a ride, no matter how little his car was, she thought bitterly. The man next to her took long strides without any emotion on his face. She could hardly keep up with him. Andrasy did not care, he had made his catch. He wondered where Toth would come into the picture. He was the only one who knew where they were supposed to go, and where the money was coming from. They owed him a bunch already. He had plans for that. Big plans.

     The train pulled into the station almost noiselessly. The electric locomotives used in most of Austria were quiet and powerful. The steep tracks hovered around mountainsides and went into them frequently. The long tunnels were just not practical for steam engines. The screeching halt of the train made her look up, searching for an entrance. The open coach was divided into comfortable benches facing each other. Only the heads of the passengers were visible in the next cubicle. She took the window seat, facing the direction of the ride. Andrasy plopped down across from her. They still did not talk.

Erika gave up totally. The urgent drive that had made her run away from her past dissipated in thin air, up, towards the very top of the majestic Alps that surrounded her, taking her last slim hope away. For she was sure that there would be no grandpa waiting for her, only her punishment for her horrid crime. The dark devils will get her after all. No one would save her now. Ken had dropped her like useless baggage, an unnecessary burden on his managerial shoulders. The Commandant had lost his appetite for individual care; feeding and clothing the multitude of refugees, spreading his time to serve the great cause must have satisfied him. Guess he was trained to do just that. Not a bit more.

Erika wished now that she could have said farewell to Theresa, and Imre and at least some of the people who were nice to her. But she had been whisked away to her doom, no one lifting a finger to save her. She decided not to cry, not any more. It would have been useless. She glanced back at the mountains as they were moving away slowly on both sides of the valley; only the Inn River stayed close to the tracks, eagerly racing against man and his modern machine.

As the valley widened, small hamlets, then bigger towns zoomed by the silvery train streaking toward the eastern part of the country. Erika saw, but did not register the stations where they made short stops; the few passengers coming and going were not even noticed. Andrasy lay back against his seat, but with his eyelids low he kept vigilance on his prey. There was no time now to snooze, and no sign of Toth.

Most of the passengers stood up and began to move toward the exits as the train slowly rolled into the enormous station of Salzburg. Erika did not recognize the place in daylight. Her first trip through here only a few months ago had seemed to happen in another life. The train rested, no new passengers entered their coach. When finally the entrance door opened, Andrasy instinctively looked up. Two Austrian policemen approached. From the other end of the coach two more were heading their way. One, perhaps with the highest rank, stopped at the end of the benches, first glancing at a photograph in his hand, then looked up. "Count Andrasy?" It definitely had an Austrian accent, definitely serious.

Erika could not comprehend the proceedings, or the fast garble of German firing back and forth. She only saw the handcuffs wiggling on Andrasy's struggling wrists as he was dragged by his shoulders off the train. When the commotion reached the second stall, the angry, loud Hungarian words made her listen up.

"You despicable son of a bitch!" Andrasy shouted at the tall skinny man in a drab raincoat. "You communist traitor! You stinking proletarian! All you wanted is the money for yourself! That is why you turned me in. You will not get away with this!" Then without lowering his tone, Andrasy continued in German. The surprised police hastily put another pair of handcuffs on Paul Toth, and dragged their second prisoner along. Erika gasped in silence. When the last officer of the group turned to her and reached out an arm, she knew that the gesture and the one word invitation "*Fraulein,*" was meant for her.

Most people on the outside platform stayed in the distance but were curious. The string of policemen and the few civilians did not give much information. As Erika stopped momentarily at the top of the stairs, a smiling face greeted her. The uniformed man of the American Red Cross just stood there, his arms raised high, his eyes blinking the happy message, 'See? I did it! I keep my promises!'

There was no need for an explanation now. She kissed his face, both sides, he searched for her lips. Again and again.

"What now?" Erika asked, "Are we going back to camp?"

"No, Darling. I am, but you are not. You are going to America. It is not safe here for you." He had his arm around her shoulder, walking toward the exit of the station. He could not tell if his sweetheart was happy or not. He did not dare ask, for he was not happy at all. Avoiding her major catastrophe, as challenging as it was, did not lessen the sad feeling that they must part again.

"You are going to Camp Kilmer in New Jersey. Mother will pick you up there. I have to stay here a bit more, there is work to do, you know." He went on about what the proceedings would be, the paperwork and interrogations by the Immigration people and all that. Then he stopped before they got into the Fiat and turned her to face him.

"So, Mrs. Williams, still want to marry me?"

"I thought you asked me before."

"Well, I'll ask you again. Do you?"

She reached up with both hands and pulled him down to be kissed.

"Great! That's great! As soon as you graduate from high school!"

"Anytime. Anywhere. How about now?"

She knew that 'now' would be another two years away. The present is painful but full of hope, and promise.
Like he promised that he would come back, and he did. To marry her, he promised twice.

He took her to one of the largest refugee camps operated by the American Red Cross, Camp Roeder. The huge facility outside the city of Salzburg, once an American military base from the Second World War, could facilitate thousands of people at once. With the help of the military, the operation served busloads of people around the clock, provided medical checkups, even treatment if needed Food rations were dispersed sometimes faster than the planes from the states could replenish them. Large recreation halls were turned into temporary lodgings where dozens of beds changed occupants almost daily. But the place was still the most coveted destination point for thousands of Hungarians, for this was where the Immigration Service processed their paperwork, investigated their backgrounds, and approved their dreams to become Americans.

Ken Williams introduced his protégé to the official at the first station of the process. She could not quite hear or understand the English that was faster than she could comprehend. The quick exchange of information, a lot of nodding, intersected by plenty of "Okays," was void of smiles. It was a very official business, Ken standing next to the official with his Red Cross cap in his hands, occasionally glancing toward Erika who was standing a distance away.

"I must go now," Ken finally walked over. "You are in good hands. By tomorrow afternoon you'll be on the plane to America. Now, do you want to kiss me again, or something?"

She did, and they did, and the official turned away to sharpen a pencil.

Erika stayed in limbo for the last few hours she was in Europe. But time flew fast. Interrogations by professional interpreters and inspections by medical personnel were new experiences. If she could only peek down from her clouds, the clouds of sheer happiness. To take the final journey alone seemed minor, the stretch of time away from her Ken bearable. She only hoped that she could just speed up time for the next two years to get through it that much sooner.

*　*　*

The large military transport plane towered over the single file of refugees. Its silver gray fuselage covered most of the horizon in front of them. The four propellers hummed through the warm up process. The line approached the boarding steps leading several stories up. And there he was, a very large soldier at the bottom of the stairs, his face pitch black, his white-gloved hands waving them on.

"Welcome to America," he repeated softly to each and every person passing him.

'But we are in Munich, Germany. Why is he saying that?' Then she remembered the stories filling the long idle hours in the refugee camps; the stories about pregnant women jumping into limousines that flew the small red-white-blue American flag at the traffic lights on the streets of Eastern Block cities, to deliver their babies on American soil. Because inside that car, it was America. And the similar stories of babies being born in-flight to the United States on Army transport planes, and having a friendly quarrel about citizenship with the country that the plane happened to fly over at that precious moment. In most cases, the baby had both. The world in the days of the Cold War was warmed with such pleasant stories.

The line moved on slowly, the steps to the plane full of excited new immigrants. The young family of three directly in front of Erika reached the greeting soldier. The little boy, about four, looked up in awe at the towering uniform. After a second or so he approached the steps. From the second landing he carefully turned back and got face to face with this unbelievable new sight. Then slowly, with adult deliberation, he licked his index finger and gently rubbed the surprised man's face.

"Mama!" he shouted with delight, "Mama! Look, it's real! It is real! It's not shoe polish." He looked at the black soldier again, then at his finger. Reassured, he climbed the stairs.

'Is there a smear test for America?' Erika thought. 'Is America real, or just something poor Eastern Europeans dream about?' By then she was there. In America. All she had to do was find her seat on the plane, and her place in that new world. And wait for her Ken Williams.

The End

THIS IS NOT THE END OF THE STORY...

...because life goes on. We all struggle to survive, to progress, to propagate, to succeed. So did Erika fifty years ago. Her story must be told, not only because you are interested to know what happened to her, but also because America became one of the strongest, richest, most coveted land on earth in part by immigrants, legal or otherwise.

Today, not like in our story of long ago, millions of foreigners are breaking laws and risking their lives just to be part of our world. They too struggle to survive and succeed. Politics and public opinion are not supporting our 'illegal' population, but, like always, America needs people who are willing to work mundane jobs for the least amounts of benefits, just because that is all that they are capable of or allowed to do.

Erika's second story has no title yet, but will be available, probably by the end of 2006. If you have ordered the "first half" of this novel, or purchased it at one of our book-signing affairs, your address information is in our file.

If you wish, please send your comments or questions to our e-mail: ajgergely@juno.com, and we'll be in touch.

Thank you for your interest and support.

Arpad J. Gergely